FINDING MR

A

David Rho

SPCK

First published in Great Britain in 2015

Society for Promoting Christian Knowledge
36 Causton Street
London SW1P 4ST
www.spckpublishing.co.uk

British Library Cataloguing-in-Publication Data
A catalogue record for this book is available from the British Library

ISBN 978–0–281–07332–0
eBook ISBN 978–0–281–07333–7

Typeset by Graphicraft Limited, Hong Kong
First printed in Great Britain by Ashford Colour Press
Subsequently digitally printed in Great Britain

eBook by Graphicraft Limited, Hong Kong

Produced on paper from sustainable forests

To Rosie

Contents

Part 1

Paradise lost	3
Bad news	14
Going home	22
A grim discovery	27
The hunter	34
Another man's shoes	40

Part 2

The sea	53
The storm	60
The lost boy	65
The wonderful day	73
A very good man	80
The rescue	87
An unexpected outcome	98
The crocodile man	106
The window cleaner	112
Disaster	118
The high tower	125

Part 3

Fields of death	133
The tree	138
The reckoning	143
Burning questions	149
Surprise encounters	156
The song of your soul	166

Part 1

Paradise lost

Had he known the hour of his death, Harry Goldman might have arranged his day rather differently. He might have made one or two phone calls to say goodbye to friends. And several more to make peace with his enemies.

If it had been in his nature, he might have said a grateful farewell to Johnson, his long-suffering butler, and perhaps given a small leaving gift to each of the staff at the big house.

On such a beautiful morning, he might have taken a stroll through the gardens with their neat gravel paths that were raked each day. He might even have admired the roses, which happened to be particularly fine that year.

But he did none of those things. Instead he went to church, which was most unusual considering it was a Thursday and Goldman detested religion. It was ironic, people said later, in view of the events about to unfold.

The day began with breakfast on the terrace: black coffee served in an elegant silver pot and slices of toast. The *Financial Times* had been placed carefully on a side table within easy reach, together with a printout of the night's Far East trading figures.

Goldman sipped his coffee and glanced thoughtfully at the financial reports. The Hang Seng Index was higher. Commodities were doing better than expected. It was all very satisfactory.

'Is he still there?' he said without looking up.

'I'm afraid so,' said Johnson with a quiet dignity, as though commenting on a matter of private grief.

'Well, sort the bastard out,' snapped Goldman. 'And do it properly this time. It's his last chance. Make sure he knows that.'

Johnson bowed and withdrew silently.

Goldman brushed a crumb from his dark grey Savile Row suit and adjusted his blue silk tie, his plump fingers hesitating for a moment on the soft fabric. For some reason he never felt entirely comfortable in his expensive clothes. It was as though they belonged to someone else.

The butler walked slowly and deliberately down the long gravel drive. The morning sun was warm on his grey hair. It was going to be another hot day – hot enough for a storm. 'You're going to get it today, sonny boy,' he muttered to himself. 'You're really going to get it.'

In the distance, across the lawns, he saw a security guard with a Dobermann on a leash patrolling the perimeter wall. The guard glanced towards the butler but gave no sign of greeting or recognition. The dog and its handler made Johnson uneasy.

As he neared the wrought-iron gates he took a small control pad from his pocket and pressed a button. The gates swung silently open. Stepping into the lane, Johnson confronted a tramp sitting with his back against one of the large stone gateposts. Beside him was a stick cut from a tree branch.

The tramp looked up, shading his eyes against the bright sunlight. 'Good morning,' he said cheerily. 'How are you today?'

The butler ignored the question. 'Are you going to push off?' he demanded. 'This is your last chance.'

'I don't think so,' said the tramp with an amiable smile.

'Then you're going to get a good hiding,' said Johnson irritably. He grabbed the stick and began to beat him about the head and shoulders. The tramp rolled over in the grass trying to dodge the blows.

Eventually the butler threw the stick down and stood back, wheezing from the exertion. 'The boss says he wants you gone,' he said. 'And so do I. Why can't you stop this nonsense? You make the place look untidy, coming here every day like this.'

'I'll go,' said the tramp, rubbing his head where the last blows had landed, 'but not until I've seen him. I've told you, there's something important he needs to know. The way things are going, your boss is heading for trouble.'

'You know nothing about his affairs,' the butler said, 'and what he does is absolutely no concern of yours. He'll see you in hell before he lets you across his doorstep, so get that into your thick head and go away. Then we can all have some peace.' He paused. 'Who are you, anyway?'

'Sheppard,' said the tramp. 'And according to people like your boss, I'm just a nobody.'

'Well, listen, Sheppard, here's a fiver – just take it and get lost. For my sake,' he added, a note of desperation in his voice.

'Sorry, Johnson, but it's not as straightforward as that. And your fiver's not the money I'm interested in. Though I do appreciate the gesture.' The tramp got to his feet and picked up the stick. 'You can tell him I'm going.'

'And you're not coming back?'

'What do you think?'

'I think you're a young fool. One day something serious is going to happen if you carry on making him angry like this.'

'What's he going to do – have me arrested?'

'The boss doesn't need the police. He's got his own way of dealing with people like you. Unpleasant ways. So, unless you can run faster than a Dobermann, you'd better go away and stay away.'

'You know, I almost think you care about me,' said the tramp with a smile. 'Maybe you're not such a bad guy after all.'

The butler glanced anxiously at the security camera on the gatepost and stepped closer to Sheppard. 'Listen,' he said in a low voice. 'The boss has cameras everywhere, so I had to make it look as though I was hitting you good and hard, or I'd be in trouble myself. That man's got a mean temper, believe me. That's why I'm telling you to go away. It's for your own good. How old are you? Thirty? Thirty-five? I've got a son your age. You've got your life in front of you. Do yourself a favour; go and get a job or something. I tell you, the boss is the wrong person to mess with.'

'And there was me thinking you didn't hit me so hard because you're an old man and past it,' said Sheppard.

'Old?' snapped the butler. 'Come back here tomorrow and you'll find out how hard I can hit. Listen, I'm being serious, the boss is bad news for people like you.'

'Johnson, believe me, I do take it seriously – but whether I'll be back tomorrow or not remains to be seen.'

As he spoke, a small red car crunched softly down the drive and out into the lane. In it were two young women with heavy make-up. They were dressed as though they had been to a party. A wild party.

'Looks as though your boss was having a good time last night. He certainly likes his creature comforts,' said Sheppard as he glimpsed a low-cut dress and bare flesh through the open car window.

'Don't even go there,' muttered Johnson.

'No, perhaps not,' said the tramp with a grin. 'Anyway, you take care of yourself.' He walked off down the lane, limping slightly as he went.

The butler stood watching until he was out of sight. Suddenly his phone rang.

'Are you going to be all day?' said a rasping voice. 'Get back here. I need the car.'

Johnson sighed wearily. He was not sure which car Mr Goldman wanted today. Maybe the Bentley again?

When he got back to the house Goldman was on the phone. An international call. The phone was on speaker and Goldman paced about the room, shouting instructions. 'Just get rid of them, Atkins, and do it soon,' he yelled. 'Clear the bastards out.'

A distant voice responded from the phone console. 'That's not going to be easy, Mr Goldman. We're talking about whole villages. Where are we going to put these people? There are hundreds of them with nowhere to go.'

'I don't care how many of them there are,' shouted Goldman. 'Just clear them out. Use the heavy gear. Get the bulldozers in. We need that land and we need it now.'

Johnson withdrew discreetly to the other side of the room and busied himself rearranging the magazines on a coffee table, trying to avoid eye contact with his boss.

Atkins, their head of operations in South America, spoke again. 'We also have an issue with publicity, Mr Goldman. And there's another problem. There's a nun.'

'What the hell do you mean, a nun?'

'She's stirring things up with the peasants. Going on about human rights. Talking to a TV crew that's hanging around. It's not going to look good in the press.'

'I don't care about the press, Atkins. All I care about is that land, and I'm not going to be messed around by a bunch of natives and a blasted nun. I want the land cleared. I don't care who lives on it; I want them out. And that includes Mother bloody Teresa. Make it happen, Atkins, or it'll be you that's out. Got that?'

'We'll certainly try, sir,' said the voice on the phone.

'Try?' yelled Goldman. 'You'll do more than try, you moron. You'll fix it, or I'll fix you. I made you and I can damn well break you. Remember that.' He leaned over the large mahogany desk and stabbed a button on the phone console. The line went dead before Atkins could reply.

Goldman turned and kicked out savagely at a chair. It crashed backwards onto the carpet. For a few moments he stood breathing heavily like an enraged bull, perspiration glistening on his forehead. Gradually, his breathing steadied and he seemed calmer.

'Huh,' he mumbled as though coming out of a bad dream. 'Useless fool.' He glanced at his watch. For a moment he hesitated, as though a thought had struck him. Then he was himself again.

'Has Henshaw brought the car round?' he demanded.

'At the door, Mr Goldman,' said Johnson from across the room.

'Good. I'm going to be out all day.' He paused. 'In fact, now I think about it, you may as well come too. We're going to church,' he said with an unexpected smile. 'And after that I've a meeting in the City.'

His anger had subsided as quickly as it had appeared, but Johnson knew better than to assume his employer would stay in a good mood.

The butler looked puzzled. Church was not a word much used in Goldman's house – or his business empire, come to that.

'A small public relations exercise,' said Goldman, seeing his confusion. 'Our name in lights. In fact, better than lights.'

Johnson was none the wiser.

'We're going to the cathedral. The dedication service of a new window. My window. Paid for by me. The window's got a panel saying who's donated this small piece of English history. My name will be up there for a thousand years.' Goldman savoured the thought. 'A very satisfactory arrangement. The Dean gets a donation to his cathedral funds, and I get my name on one of the prime sites in the country. The house of God.'

* * *

As with most things Mr Goldman set his mind to, the morning went exactly to plan.

While he was inside the cathedral at the brief dedication service and the reception afterwards in the medieval chapter house, Johnson stood chatting with Henshaw in the car park. The chauffeur pulled out a packet of cigarettes and offered one to the butler.

Johnson shook his head. 'He'll have a fit if he catches you.'

'Evil little swine,' said Henshaw, lighting up. He drew deeply on the cigarette, savouring the effect of the nicotine, then blew the smoke down both nostrils.

'He's not so little,' replied Johnson. 'It's the way he walks. Stooping, as though there's something wrong with his spine.'

'That's because he's always reaching out, grasping for more money. Grabbing at everything he can get his greedy hands on. Hunchback of Tresco Towers, that's him,' said Henshaw. 'I hate his sort.'

'You could always leave,' said Johnson.

Henshaw pulled strongly on the cigarette. 'Yes? And where am I going to get another job at my age? Or you, come to that? No, mate, we're stuck with the bastard.'

The conversation was interrupted by voices as Goldman emerged from the chapter house and made his farewells.

'Blast,' muttered Henshaw, hurriedly treading his cigarette into the ground and putting his chauffeur's peaked cap back on. He opened the rear door of the Bentley ready for Goldman, saluting as his employer approached.

Goldman strode up and held out his hand.

'Sir?' said Henshaw, confused.

'You know what.'

Henshaw silently handed over the cigarettes and lighter.

'And the car keys,' snarled Goldman. 'You're sacked.'

'Sir?'

'And I'll have your fancy hat and jacket as well,' said Goldman, a vein throbbing in his temple. Goldman passed the keys to Johnson. 'Drive,' he said.

'But what about me, sir?' pleaded Henshaw.

'What about you, sir? You can damn well walk.'

Goldman got into the back of the car and slammed the heavy door. It gave a satisfying 'clunk' as it closed, sealing him off from the outside world. Relaxing in the soft leather upholstery of the Bentley as it cruised through the lush countryside, Goldman forgot about the incident with Henshaw. Instead he was thinking about the cathedral and its very patrician Dean.

A kindred spirit, he reflected. A man of the world. A man who appreciated money and power. A man on the inside. A man who might be useful.

It had all gone very well. Except for the realization that it was the first time he had been inside a church since his wedding. He thought back to his brief marriage to Trudi, the confident New Yorker he had met on a business trip to the States; their few months of happiness. Perhaps pleasure would have been a better word.

In her teens she had trained at ballet school, and twenty years later still walked with the easy grace of a dancer. She had skin that glowed and a body that aroused desire among men and envy in women. Goldman had been proud to be seen in her company. They had been good together. At first.

Then, gradually, it began to fall apart. Trudi was always on about going home to Manhattan.

'Harry, I'm sick of this English weather,' she complained. 'Nothing but rain and fog. And this goddam house, stuck out here in the middle of nowhere. I'm a city girl, Harry. I like dancing. I need action. All we got round here is fields and cows. And the only person

I get to talk to is the cleaner woman. Sometimes I think she's the only one who really cares about me. And you – you don't really love me, Harry. All you care about is money. It's like I'm married to a machine. I don't know what makes you this way, but it's drivin' me nuts.'

Being pregnant only made matters worse, and it certainly took the edge off sex – although that had always tended to be unsatisfying.

'I feel fat, Harry. And my back. Jeez, my back aches real bad. I wanna go home, Harry. I need my mom.'

For Goldman the thrill of being married to a beautiful, leggy blonde faded into normality; then soured into resentment. At five foot ten she was a good inch taller than him. At first they'd laughed about it but Goldman, who felt short and plump in comparison, hated looking up to anyone.

Finally, Trudi got her own way. She went home to Mom and never returned. The child, a boy, was born in New York. But by then they were drifting silently out of each other's lives.

The birth brought back bitter memories of his own childhood – memories he struggled to forget. Memories that sometimes crept up on him in the night, slipping silently into his dreams, even after all those years.

Goldman never set eyes on this small bringer of fear, and had no wish to. In any case, it was her child. She wanted it: she could damn well keep it. Once she sent him a photograph. A baby in a cot covered with a blue blanket. Blue for a boy. On the back she had written just two words: 'Your Son.'

Her handwriting was strong and stylish – just like her. He ripped the photograph up and threw it in the wastepaper basket. One piece of the picture fell on the carpet, but he did not notice.

Later that day, when Goldman had gone to dinner, the cleaner emptied the wastepaper basket and saw the torn fragment on the floor. She picked it up and studied it thoughtfully for a moment. She sighed softly to herself, then carried on with the cleaning.

That night, when the dreams were bad again, Goldman woke and went back to retrieve the torn-up photograph, but the wastepaper basket was empty.

Six months later came the letter. It was postmarked New York. In it was a plain white card with the words: 'Our baby died. Cot death. Trudi.' The handwriting was clear and confident and gave no indication of her grief.

He had not replied. She was no longer of use to him and so he had no interest in her. The parting of the ways had been sudden and complete. In the absence of any further domestic complications, Goldman turned his attention back to the world of business and finance. The place where he belonged.

Now it was as it had been before they met. Straightforward.

Goldman glanced out of the car window at the passing countryside. He had thought all that was in the past, but something in the cathedral had caught him unawares. For a moment the calm of the ancient building had felt chill, as though his sleeve had been gently tugged by an unseen hand.

Goldman shook his head to clear his mind of such thoughts. His phone rang. It was Atkins again.

Johnson stared ahead through the windscreen, pretending to be unaware of Goldman's anger as he bellowed at their man in South America.

'She what? How can she be? I only spoke to you a few hours ago. Who told the damn fools to kill her?' He paused while Atkins spoke. 'Well, that's your problem, not mine,' snapped Goldman. 'I never told you to do that. You fix it with the press. I want results and I don't care how you get them.'

Goldman tossed the phone down on the seat beside him. He gave a low growl. Atkins was dead meat. And he wasn't the only one. Goldman felt the anger rising within him. The anger made him strong: made him dangerous.

He thought about the meeting in the City. Two more hours and yet another company would be his. Their board of directors would scream and shout, but the bastards were screwed, and they knew it. The takeover battle had been brutal and bloody. Like two wrestlers fighting it out in the ring, grappling and gouging until the stronger triumphs. The weaker one submits; the struggle is over.

Goldman smiled grimly to himself, his fists clenched in triumph. This was his moment of victory. They were being forced to submit. But he wouldn't just defeat them. He would destroy them.

The idea excited him. His laughter was harsh like the cry of a hawk.

He leaned forward to order Johnson to drive faster, but for some reason the words would not form in his head. He had a sense of detachment. He realized he was sweating.

He looked at his watch; the gold second hand moved relentlessly like a ratchet, eating up the minutes. He felt uneasy. Fearful. Was there something he had forgotten? He undid the metal bracelet of the watch.

He glanced up almost absent-mindedly at Johnson in the front. He felt no pain as the steady pumping of his heart tripped abruptly into a rapid, irregular pattern. There was a fluttering sensation in his chest, like a bird startled by danger.

His heart resumed its regular beat. Goldman sighed, but not with contentment. He was perspiring heavily now. His shirt was wet under his immaculately tailored suit, his face running with sweat.

He opened his mouth, but he could not remember what he was going to say. He was feeling distant from it all, as though he was travelling down a long, dark tunnel.

There was pressure in his chest that tightened with each movement of the second hand on the watch. He reached forward to attract Johnson's attention.

Suddenly there was a burning pain. It flooded up inside him, pressing hard against his throat, ramming his head back and arching his spine so he thought it would snap. He cried out in agony, but no sound came.

Fire broke through, bursting into his skull. His eyes were wide with fear but he could see nothing but whiteness. The Rolex fell silently onto the carpet at Goldman's feet.

Everything was completely still.

* * *

Goldman was not sure what happened next. The trees outside the car were no longer moving. In fact there was no sign of the car. The pain

12

in his chest had gone. It felt like a dream – but not the dreams that came to him in the night.

He found himself on his feet, standing under some trees near the bank of a river. The river was wide and the current slow. He took a deep breath, like a baby lifted new-born from the womb.

It was then that he realized he was dead.

Instinctively he reached for his phone, but it was not there. With a sinking feeling he remembered he had left it on the back seat of the car with the order of service from the cathedral. Apart from an almost empty wallet, all he had on him were Henshaw's cigarettes and lighter.

'Damn,' he said.

Bad news

Goldman looked round uncertainly. Standing a few feet away was a shabbily dressed man. He was wearing a dark blue jacket that might once have been part of a suit and a pair of old jeans, worn thin at the knees. Goldman glimpsed what appeared to be grubby bindings on his wrists.

The tramp looked vaguely familiar. He was talking to a fair-haired young man who was carefully studying a clipboard. The younger man wore a cream linen suit and a blue open-neck shirt that seemed to reflect the colour of the cloudless sky. His battered panama had seen better days, but still managed to look stylish. A young tortoiseshell cat was rubbing itself against his leg, demanding attention.

The young man glanced up from the clipboard, as though Goldman had spoken. 'Is anything wrong?' he asked, seeing the frown on Goldman's face. 'You look unhappy.'

'Never mind whether I'm happy or not,' retorted Goldman. 'What the bloody hell's going on? Where am I? And who in hell's name are you?'

'Yes, it comes as a bit of a shock,' said the young man in a polite tone. 'According to my notes, you had a heart attack. Not much by way of advance warning, I admit, but there it is. These things happen,' he said sympathetically. 'And who am I? Well, my name's Raphael but people usually call me Raffa. I'm a sort of gatekeeper. It's only admin grade, but I enjoy the work. I meet some interesting people. I'm here to start you off on your journey.'

'Journey? What journey?' demanded Goldman in alarm.

'Ah, yes. Let me explain. When people die they go to . . .' Raffa paused as though taking particular care over his next words. 'When people die, they pass on . . . It may sound improbable, but there we

14

are. Our presentational skills have not always been of the best. Let me put it this way: when you die, life doesn't stop. In fact, it gets even better. For most people, anyway. So it's all quite positive, despite the bad press we seem to receive. Try to think of it as a beginning rather than the end.'

He paused as he saw the frown on Goldman's face. 'Oh dear, I can see you're not entirely convinced. Look – it's all very straightforward. All you have to do is walk across the river. The stepping stones are large and the water's not very deep. Florence does it all the time.'

'Who the hell is Florence?' demanded Goldman.

'This is Florence,' said Raffa, bending to stroke the cat, which arched its back in appreciation.

'As I said, it's quite straightforward,' he continued. 'You simply walk across to the other side. And there you are – the future is open before you. Now, which of you is first, you or your friend Mr Sheppard here?'

'Friend?' snapped Goldman. 'This deadbeat's no damn friend of mine. And I'm going over first.'

Goldman's hands were clenched as though gripping something very tightly. Raffa was about to continue, but Goldman cut in: 'Listen, you public school tosser, you need to know who it is you're talking to. I'm a very important man. I've built up a business empire worth millions – billions in fact. Then there's the house. Tresco, it's called. Named after a paradise island. And that's what it is for me: paradise. It's got I don't know how many bedrooms. And grounds – wonderful grounds. The roses are particularly good this year, so I'm told.'

'I must say that sounds most impressive,' said Raffa. 'Was your work commercial or industrial?'

'Both.'

'International?' ventured Raphael.

'Absolutely,' said Goldman, energized by the conversation. 'Shipping. A lot of shipping. Ore carriers, oil tankers. Then there's aviation. Air cargo mainly. We just took delivery of some new wide-bodied jets. Very profitable.'

'And would that be everything?' asked Raffa.

'Certainly not,' snapped Goldman. 'There's the mining projects. Gold, copper, bauxite – anything that's got value. Then there's the utilities. We're big there, too. Offshore gas, oil extraction in Alaska and the Middle East. Even got a stake in a couple of nuclear power facilities coming on stream. Energy: that's the future.'

'Ah, yes, the future,' echoed Raphael pensively. 'Quite amazing.'

'You're damn right it's amazing. It's a fantastic achievement. My achievement. I've created all that – created it out of nothing. It's who I am, and proud of it.'

He paused for a moment, as though deep in thought, then added, 'It's just a shame you can't take it with you when you go.'

Raffa lowered his clipboard and looked puzzled. 'Can't take it with you? Whatever gave you that idea? Of course you can. You can take all your possessions with you. In fact, we rather insist on it. The future is waiting for you over there on the other side of the river. All you do is take your possessions – everything you really value, that is, and walk across the stepping stones. As I said, it's quite straightforward.'

Goldman looked uneasy. 'You take your possessions with you?'

'Yes.'

'And carry them across the stepping stones?'

'That's it.'

'All your possessions?'

'Absolutely. As you said yourself, the things that make you who you are.'

An unpleasant thought was forming in Goldman's mind. 'But it'll take me for ever to carry everything I've got across that river.'

'Yes, I suspect that may be true,' Raffa murmured. He took off his hat as though showing respect for someone who has received distressing news. A stray wisp of straw floated to the ground. 'On the other hand, you do have plenty of time,' he said.

He turned to Sheppard, his face brightening. 'Is that stick all you've got? Well, there's nothing to stop you going across now if you want to.'

With that, the tramp set off down to the river. Somewhere in the far distance there was the sound of music and laughter. It sounded like a party was going on.

But as he reached the water's edge, Sheppard paused. He turned and looked back. Goldman, who had been shouting furiously at Raffa, was now sitting with his head in his hands. Sheppard studied him for a moment, then began to retrace his steps up the river bank.

Goldman looked up as he heard him approach. 'What have you come back for?' he demanded. 'Get lost. Leave me alone.' He paused, then muttered, 'Scum.'

'I thought you might like a bit of help finding your stuff,' said Sheppard, ignoring the insult.

'Stuff?' shouted Goldman. 'I don't have "stuff", you oaf. I have a brilliant business empire that I created. I have valuable possessions I've worked hard for. I have factories and ships and . . .' His voice trailed off into silence.

'You have a problem,' said Sheppard. 'I thought you could do with a hand finding your way.'

Goldman squinted up at him suspiciously. 'Why? Why would you do that? Why would you want to help me?'

The tramp shrugged. 'I'm in no particular hurry to get across the river. As Raffa said, we have plenty of time. I thought it might be a neighbourly thing to do.'

The other man scowled with distaste. He hesitated for a moment, then said, 'OK, but don't try anything funny.'

'Listen,' said Sheppard. 'I don't want to be rude, but you're the one with the problem. You're the one with I don't know how many tons of gear to get across that river. All I need to do is to walk across the stepping stones.'

'All right,' said Goldman grudgingly. 'But where do we start?'

Sheppard glanced round as though about to ask Raffa for guidance, but the young man with the clipboard had disappeared.

'Maybe we should try and find our own way,' he said. 'You can just see the outline of a track over there where the grass has been trodden. By the look of it other people have been this way before us. Anything's better than sitting here doing nothing.'

They were an odd-looking pair: Goldman in his expensive suit and shiny black shoes, arguing and shouting as he went; the tramp in his worn jacket and jeans. The path, such as it was, became uneven and in many places overgrown, and Goldman's expensive Italian shoes slipped on the dew that made the grass sparkle in the sunlight. Trees hung low over the track and brushed against their faces as they walked.

As the hours passed and the sun rose higher, Goldman began to perspire. 'I've got to stop for a rest,' he said eventually. 'We've walked for miles and not seen a soul. Are you sure this is the right way?'

Sheppard shrugged. 'Who knows? Maybe we need to keep walking and see where it brings us. I haven't seen another path, so we don't have a lot of choice.'

As they walked, Goldman began to sense that they were not alone. It was as though they were being watched. He felt a distant fear returning, a fear from his childhood. Of being left alone in the house on a darkening winter's afternoon. And of something else. He turned to see who was following them, but there were only trees. Got to snap out of it, he thought. Bloody nonsense. Nothing there.

Gradually the path brought them into more open country. Eventually the two men stopped to rest.

'It's no good,' said Goldman. 'This is a complete waste of time.'

'What is?'

'This walking. We've been going for hours. Now we're heading into those hills.'

'So?'

'So it's bad enough trying to walk on the flat in these shoes without going up and down mountains as well. Anyway, how are we going to get my things back to the river? It must be miles.'

'We?' said the tramp, surprised. 'What do you mean, "we"? I've only come to help you find the way. I didn't say anything about helping you carry your things. It's your precious stuff, after all.'

Goldman grabbed the tramp by the front of his jacket. 'Are you saying you won't help me, you bastard? What are you going to do – stand there and watch me struggle on my own?'

The tramp disengaged Goldman's hands from his coat. 'I was only joking. I'm simply reminding you that I don't actually have to be here with you. And you don't have a manner that encourages cooperation.'

'Meaning what?'

'That you're selfish and arrogant – something along those lines. When did you ever help anyone else?'

'Say that again and I'll flatten you,' shouted Goldman.

'Possibly,' said the tramp. 'But I'm not so sure about that. Anyway, let's not fall out this early in the relationship. I'll give you a hand with your stuff, assuming we ever find it.'

'And what am I supposed to do: go down on my knees and thank you?'

'No, but the occasional companionable word might help,' said the tramp. 'Anyway, let's push on; it'll be dark soon and we need to think about finding somewhere to sleep.'

They walked for a couple more hours. Finally, in the distance, they saw a spiral of smoke rising into the evening air. Far off in the silence a dog barked. Before long, they could make out a sprawl of houses.

'A village,' said Goldman. 'At least there'll be somewhere to stay the night.' The thought of food and shelter drew them on and they walked purposefully towards the settlement.

One of the first buildings they came to was a down-at-heel pub. Despite its mock-Tudor shabbiness, Goldman glanced appreciatively at the hanging baskets on either side of the dark wood door. There were two cars in an otherwise empty car park. 'Looks promising enough,' he murmured as they pushed open the door and went inside.

There was a faint aroma of stale beer. The bar was empty, except for two women sitting at a table next to the fireplace. The barman stared at the tramp's untidy appearance as the two men entered. 'Yes?' he said. It was more of a challenge than a welcome.

'Gin and tonic. Large,' said Goldman.

'Ice and lemon?'

'Both.'

The barman measured out a double shot of spirit. He opened a bottle of tonic and set it down on the bar beside the gin. 'And your friend?' he said with the slightest hint of irony.

'He's not a friend,' snapped Goldman. 'We happened to meet on the road.'

The barman looked in disgust at Sheppard's shabby clothes and dirty fingernails. The cuffs of his jacket were frayed and his wrists were strapped up with not very clean bandages. There was the warm smell of sweat about him. 'Well, whoever you are, what are you having to drink?'

Sheppard looked at his companion and shrugged. 'Sorry – no money.'

'I'll pay,' sighed the other. 'A beer,' he said to the barman without consulting the tramp. 'But only a half.'

They drank in silence. The women across the room were watching them and laughing. One seemed particularly interested in the two men. She was smiling, but there was something of a haunted look about her. Shadows smudged her thin face. And perhaps something else.

'She's giving me the eye,' said Goldman quietly. 'This is when you disappear and find yourself somewhere to sleep.'

'What about you?'

'Don't worry, I'll be fine. I'm sure they'll be able to find me a room.' He paused, then added, 'You don't expect me to fork out for you as well, do you?'

'Of course not,' said Sheppard, smiling. 'That's OK. I'll find somewhere to bed down.'

'And be back here bright and early in the morning,' said Goldman. 'I know your sort. Lying in bed all day, stoned out of your heads. We need to get going. I'll see you outside. Eight o'clock. On the dot. Make sure you're there.'

'I will be,' said Sheppard. 'I don't have a problem getting up in the mornings.' He finished his drink and walked to the door. The two women were still talking. Goldman stood in silence at the bar reflecting on the events of the day.

'Hello,' said a soft voice beside him.

Goldman turned to the young woman who had come over from the fireside. 'Hello,' he said, running an eye over her slim figure. She looked vaguely familiar, but he wasn't thinking about that.

'Can we talk?'

'In private?' asked Goldman thoughtfully. Her body looked soft and inviting. He caught a hint of perfume. It reminded him of something – or someone.

The woman hesitated for a moment. 'Well . . . yes, all right.'

Goldman grinned, remembering the two young hookers that had been provided for him the previous night. He felt the same violent desire rise up inside him. He turned to the barman. 'I need a room.'

'Of course, sir.' He winked as he handed Goldman a key. 'Number three – up the stairs and to your left. Sleep well, sir.'

'Don't worry, I will,' said Goldman as he put his arm round the girl's waist and guided her towards the stairs. He felt the warmth of her back through the thin material of her dress and slid his hand lower. This was more like it.

Going home

The next morning was damp and grey. Sheppard stood outside the back of the pub stamping his feet and rubbing his arms to keep warm. He knocked on the kitchen door and it was eventually opened by a plump, homely woman in a flowered apron.

'Any chance of a cup of tea?' asked the tramp.

The woman looked at him suspiciously for a moment, then said, 'Are you with him who arrived last night?'

'Sort of.'

'And where did you sleep?' she asked accusingly.

'In the shed.'

'Yes, and you look as though you did.'

Sheppard made an attempt to smooth his short, dark hair and straightened his jacket. It did not improve his appearance but it made the woman smile.

'Your friend not buying you breakfast, then?'

'I don't think so,' said Sheppard with a grin.

'No. I don't think so either,' said the woman with a look that indicated she had not formed a high opinion of Goldman. 'Wait here,' she said.

That boy's got a twinkle in those blue eyes of his, she thought to herself as she walked back into the pub. A good bath and he'd be a fine-looking lad. I'd give him a good scrub down any day . . .

She pulled herself up short. Kathleen Connolly, what are you thinking of!

A few minutes later she reappeared with a mug of tea and a brown paper package, setting them down on an empty beer keg.

'Thanks,' said Sheppard.

'Drink it while it's hot and get that bacon sandwich into you. You look thin. You sure you're all right?'

'I'm fine. Busy at the moment. A lot of travelling.'

'Well, you take care,' said the woman with a warning frown. 'And watch it with him. He's a nasty piece of work, if you ask me. Heaven only knows what he was getting up to last night. All that shouting and yelling.'

With his mouth full, Sheppard could only nod.

'Anyway,' she said, 'I need to get on before someone notices I'm away from the kitchen.' She spoke in a brisk, businesslike manner which she hoped masked her thoughts.

'I'll take care,' he said. 'And thanks for the grub. You're a sweetheart.'

She flashed him a smile, realized she was blushing, and fled in confusion back to the safety of the kitchen. As the door closed behind her, Sheppard took another drink of tea and finished the sandwich. There was nothing like a bacon butty on a foggy morning.

At exactly eight o'clock, Goldman emerged from the front door to find Sheppard waiting in the car park. 'A good night?' asked the tramp as they rejoined the path and headed towards the hills.

'Very good,' said the other man, with obvious satisfaction. 'Very good indeed.'

Sheppard glanced at him expectantly. 'And?'

'It still works.' He saw Sheppard's quizzical look. 'Last night. One of those two women sitting by the fire. I pulled.'

'Really?'

'The slim one – nice pair of knockers and a tight little arse. She came over and started chatting – and there we were.'

'You slept with her?'

'Not much sleep, but plenty of the other. Like I said, neat little body on her. A bit skinny but very invigorating.'

'You scored?' said the tramp doubtfully.

'Certainly did. And very agreeable it was too. Used the last of my cash but it was well worth it.'

'I thought you were loaded.'

'I don't carry a lot of money round with me,' said Goldman. 'I've got other people to pay for things I need.'

'Had other people,' said Sheppard.

'Whatever,' said Goldman with a shrug. 'It was still worth it.'

The events of the previous night had clearly given Goldman renewed energy and he strode out half a pace ahead.

'I don't want to appear rude,' said Sheppard limping after him, trying to keep up, 'but why would an attractive young woman like that want to sleep with you?'

Goldman stopped abruptly. 'Meaning what?' he snapped.

The tramp hesitated. 'Well, you're not exactly blessed with film-star looks. In fact you're middle-aged and going thin on top. Not to mention being a bit overweight. I wondered what the big attraction was.'

'Attraction? What's always the attraction?' said Goldman. 'Money. The world's greatest aphrodisiac. Turns women on. Women like her, anyway.'

'What sort of woman's that?'

'Tarts. Scrubbers. Girls on the game. Women who want to make a bob or two on their backs.'

'Or need to?'

'Listen, pal. They want it, I've got it. They've got it, I want it. Simple as that. A mutually attractive business arrangement.'

'So she needed the money, and you wanted a screw?'

'Putting it crudely, yes.'

'Did she enjoy it?'

Goldman looked puzzled. 'Who the hell cares about that? We both got what we wanted.'

'But did she want to do it?'

Goldman frowned slightly. 'Well, at first she was a bit reluctant, but so what – it just made things more interesting. The excitement of the chase and all that.' He paused. 'You know, I got the feeling it was her first time.' He was silent for few moments as if a thought had occurred to him. 'But it couldn't have been.'

'So what did you do when she was a bit reluctant, as you put it?' asked Sheppard.

'What do you think? Haven't you ever had an awkward one? I did what we all do and carried on regardless. She soon latched on to the idea. Well, after I gave her a good slapping she did. Maybe that's why they're called slappers,' he said and laughed.

'You mean you forced her,' said Sheppard.

'Bollocks. What is this, the Spanish Inquisition? Are you saying I raped her or something? She was up for it. She wanted the money, that's for sure. You don't take "no" from women like that. They know what the deal is. That's why she came over and started chatting me up.'

'She must have needed the money a hell of a lot.'

'That's life,' said Goldman. 'That's how things are. Get real – and get bloody walking. Otherwise we're never going to find my things.'

'I had a good night's sleep too, since you ask,' said Sheppard.

'I didn't ask and I'm not interested in how or where you slept,' retorted Goldman.

'And a good breakfast,' added the tramp, grinning. Goldman ignored him.

The tramp walked in silence a few paces behind his companion. He thought back to the two women in the bar. Especially the slim one with the haunted look.

'Strange, though,' said Goldman, turning back to the tramp. 'That woman. The hooker. She reminded me of someone, but I can't quite remember who. Funny, that. I'm usually good with faces. You, for instance. I had you worked out back at the river. You're the layabout who used to sit by the gates at Tresco making the place look a mess. Johnson should have set the damn dogs on you.'

'How do you know it was me?' said Sheppard.

'I keep my eye on things. Watched you on the security cameras – making sure Johnson did his job properly. But that woman . . . I know her from somewhere, but I can't quite place her.' His voice trailed off into a silence.

* * *

That night there was no village and no pub. As darkness fell they were in woodland. There was nothing for it but to make a fire and sleep rough. The next day would be hard going, as the path began to climb into the hills in the far distance.

As they lay in the darkness trying to sleep, Goldman seemed agitated. 'Can you hear something?' he whispered.

'What?' said Sheppard.

'I don't know. Something. Out there in the bushes. I think we're being watched.'

'Could be a rabbit,' said the tramp. 'I don't know. Things come out to look for food in the night. Maybe it's a badger. Go to sleep.'

'No, it's more than that. Something big.'

Sheppard groaned. 'Perhaps it's an elephant. Use your phone. Make a long-distance call. Anything. Just go to sleep.'

'I haven't got my phone,' said Goldman. 'I left it in the bloody car.'

There was silence. Before long he could hear Sheppard's gentle snores. Goldman lay awake for a long time, struggling with the fear that seemed to be creeping towards him in the darkness. For the first time in years he felt vulnerable. Afraid.

He wished Johnson was there to bring him a cup of coffee, or that he was back in bed with the hooker with the soft, warm body and the perfume that had seemed vaguely familiar. Anywhere but in a dark, damp wood with some creature out there watching him.

A grim discovery

The warmth of the morning sun woke them. They rose, stiff from sleeping on the hard ground, and set off with hardly a word. This time Goldman lagged behind, still resentful that the tramp had not taken his fear of the night before seriously.

It was about midday when he stopped abruptly. The tramp turned to see what was wrong. 'I recognize this place,' said Goldman slowly. 'I've been here before. We're only a few miles from Tresco, I'm sure of it.'

But what he judged to be a few miles turned out to be a lot more when it came to walking instead of being swept along in the back of a Bentley. So it was not until late in the day that they saw ahead of them the mansion with its wrought-iron gates.

Except that, as they drew nearer, they realized that things had changed dramatically in the time they had been away. Goldman stopped and clasped his hand to his mouth, moaning as if he was in pain. Suddenly he dropped his hand and bellowed: 'No, no – NO!'

The shout of rage echoed across the empty fields. As they approached the imposing entrance, they saw that the ornate gates were thick with rust. The security camera had been ripped from the stone gatepost, the wiring hanging lifeless like tendons wrenched from a dismembered corpse.

The two men struggled to push open the heavy gates. Inside, the lawns were overgrown, rotting leaves were turning to a black sludge in the broken fountain and weeds grew in the gravel of the drive. Goldman walked like a man in a dream, his eyes wide with shock. Most of the windows in the house had been smashed and graffiti was sprayed in grotesque patterns across the golden sandstone of the walls.

The two men called, 'Hello?' But no answer came. There was no sign of the gardeners, the security guards – or of Johnson. The place was deserted.

'There was a time I thought I'd never get in here,' said the tramp. Goldman scowled at him but did not reply.

The front door seemed jammed and it took them some minutes to force it open. Only then did the full extent of the desolation hit them. Thick dust and cobwebs covered everything. A malevolent grey fungus had crept over the oak panelling of the walls and the floor was littered with bird droppings. Sheppard wrinkled his nose at the smell of damp and decay. There was no sign of any of the staff.

Goldman ran his hand over the banister rail of the great staircase, as if caressing the body of someone he loved. It was encrusted with dirt and he recoiled in disgust. 'What the hell's happened?' he said, as much to himself as to the tramp. He seemed at a loss. 'I was here a few days ago. This place was beautiful, clean, full of people. But look at it now. It's a bloody ruin.'

'Maybe it was more than a few days ago,' said Sheppard.

'What do you mean by that?'

'It seems only a short time for us, but maybe it's different here. Years instead of days. Or . . .' he paused. 'Something else.'

'What are you going on about?' demanded Goldman, his anger returning.

'Well, I'm not sure you're going to like it, but I was thinking, maybe this is what the place was always like – under the surface. Underneath all the trappings of . . . I don't know, wealth. The money, the butler, the gardeners, the posh cars.'

'Are you saying I lived in a shit-hole like this?' snapped Goldman. 'You stupid bastard. I lived in a beautiful, wonderful house.'

'Wonderful to you, maybe,' said Sheppard, 'but at what cost to other people? I'm not trying to attack you, I'm just saying that beauty built on the pain of others seems really quite, well, ugly.'

Goldman did not reply. They stood for a long time in a tense silence as they contemplated the devastation around them. Finally, Sheppard said, 'Listen, I know this is terrible, but we've got work to do. Let's try to concentrate on that. It might even make things a bit easier. What do you want to take first?'

'Take?' said Goldman, as though not understanding what was being said.

'That's why we've come back, isn't it? What are we going to start carrying to the river?'

Goldman seemed confused. Then, gradually, he came to his senses. 'The money. We need to take the money first. It's upstairs – in the safe. At least, it was in the safe.'

He walked slowly up the long staircase like a man going to the gallows. The tramp followed in silence. There was a scuffling as a mouse bolted for safety. They walked along an empty corridor and eventually came to a large room. It was in darkness. Goldman walked across to draw back the heavy velvet curtains. As he pulled on the rich material the heavy brass curtain rail came away from the wall and crashed down, showering him in a cloud of choking dust and cobwebs.

A fly buzzed frantically against one of the few unbroken windows, desperate to escape into the fresh air. Weak sunlight filtered into the room, revealing furniture that appeared to have been abandoned years ago. A large desk was covered with grime. A pile of papers had turned yellow with age. A chair lay on its back on the carpet. The phone had been ripped out and thrown against a wall. A rusting filing cabinet stood open. More papers littered the floor.

'This is not possible,' said Goldman as though in a dream. 'This can't be happening.' He was aware of the tramp watching him. Calmly, patiently. The tramp reminded him of someone, but he couldn't think who.

Goldman walked over to a mahogany door and turned the handle. The door swung open, revealing a strongroom. He studied the dial on the inner steel door and thought for a moment. Then he carefully keyed in a number. The hinges were stiff but the heavy door opened. Unexpectedly a light came on. Inside, on the left of the strongroom, were neat stacks of bright yellow ingots. On the other side stood a large gunmetal-grey cabinet with numbered drawers.

Goldman glanced over his shoulder. 'It's still here,' he said. 'At least they haven't taken the money.'

'Who?'

Goldman shook his head. 'I don't know. The swine who wrecked the house.'

The tramp waited patiently as Goldman struggled to carry the heavy ingots out of the strongroom and stack them on the faded carpet.

'What are you doing?' he asked.

'Getting the stuff,' said Goldman. 'Like you said.'

'And how many of those bars do you think we'll be able to carry?'

Goldman sat down, confused. 'Shit. I never thought of that.'

'Look, it doesn't matter what we take first,' said the tramp. 'It's all got to go.'

'We'll take the money first,' said Goldman, getting to his feet and starting to carry the gold bars back into the strongroom. 'Otherwise someone will steal it.'

'Who on earth's going to steal it?' said the tramp. 'There's no one here, and in any case it's tucked up nice and snug in your big safe.'

Goldman carried the last of the gold bars back into the strongroom and stood panting with the exertion for a few moments. Then he opened one of the drawers in the steel cabinet. It was full of coins. There was a pile of neatly folded canvas bags in one corner of the strongroom and he started to fill them.

'What are they?' asked the tramp.

'Krugers. Safest way to hold money.'

'More gold,' muttered the tramp miserably. 'Why couldn't it be dollar bills? Or travellers' cheques. Paper would be easier to carry.'

It took Goldman a long time to fill the bags. His hands seemed to caress the shining yellow coins as he scooped them up. When he had filled four of the bags with as many coins as they thought they could manage, he closed the strongroom door and locked it.

Heading back down the staircase, Goldman fought back tears of rage. 'I can't believe it,' he said. 'It's a bloody nightmare.'

'Talking of nightmares, have you thought how we're going to carry this stuff?' asked Sheppard. 'We need some rope or something to make handles with – we can't walk around clutching these bags like strangled chickens. Anyway, I need to be able to sling one over my shoulder to leave a hand free for my stick.'

Goldman looked round vaguely. 'Rope? No – never seen anything like that in the house.'

'Maybe these curtain cords, then?' suggested Sheppard. He walked over to the window. 'I don't suppose you've got a knife?'

'Sorry.'

'Well, maybe we could burn through the cords,' said Sheppard.

'I've got a lighter,' said Goldman.

As the tramp applied Henshaw's cigarette lighter to the curtain cords, the dust on the curtains flared up in a shower of tiny sparks. Sheppard beat them out hurriedly and wiped his blackened hands on his jeans.

The makeshift handles were not perfect but they seemed to work. They stepped outside and Goldman dragged the heavy front door shut behind them. As it closed there was a gentle gust of wind as though the house sighed. Goldman stood for a moment, as if saying goodbye to an old friend. He pulled out his handkerchief and wiped his eyes.

The gravel crunched under their feet as they walked back down the drive. Looking across the overgrown lawns they could see, in the distance, acres of parkland that were rapidly reverting to wilderness.

After an hour's walking, they were aching from their unaccustomed burden. Eventually Goldman stopped and examined the palms of his hands where the weight of the bags had cut into the soft flesh. 'I'm getting blisters,' he said pathetically.

He looked back the way they had come. In the distance there was a pall of black smoke that drifted slowly in the evening breeze. 'What the hell's that?' he said. Then he turned on the tramp. 'It's Tresco. You've set my bloody house on fire, you stupid bastard.'

He set off running back the way they had come, but after a few yards remembered the bags. He retraced his steps and grabbed the money – then gave a howl of frustration as he realized he was unable to run and carry the heavy bags at the same time.

By the time they got back to Tresco, the house was a blazing inferno. As they watched helplessly, Goldman saw smoke curling against the glass of one of the last remaining windows. Suddenly there was a dull rumble and the roof collapsed in a great shower of sparks. Air, sucked in through the broken windows, created a powerful vortex of flame that roared up through the open roof space, sending burning fragments flying across the fields.

Goldman looked at Sheppard. 'You did that,' he snarled. 'You burnt my bloody house down.'

Sheppard looked aghast. 'I'm sorry. I'm really sorry. It must have been the curtains. I thought I'd beaten all the sparks out.'

Goldman looked as though he might attack the tramp; then he slumped as the breath went out of him. 'Oh, what the hell does it matter?' he groaned. 'It was a ruin anyway.'

'And there'll be a lot less stuff to carry,' said Sheppard hopefully.

Goldman scowled at him. 'Don't push your luck.'

* * *

As they walked, they passed a woman begging at the roadside. She had a small child with her. He looked underfed. In his hand he held a piece of blue cloth which he stroked as if to comfort himself.

He stared up at the two men, unblinking. The woman was silent. Holding out her hand, she wordlessly implored the travellers for help. Putting his stick down, the tramp squatted beside her. He smiled in greeting and spoke a few quiet words, gently stroking the child's head.

Goldman strode on, avoiding eye contact and saying nothing. After a few paces, he muttered something under his breath.

'What?' asked the tramp.

'Parasites. Why don't they get a job instead of sponging off other people?'

'Assuming there is work?'

'Never done a hand's turn in their lives.'

'Do you know who they were?'

'They weren't anybody. Bloody gypsies, most likely.'

'And who are we?'

Goldman shrugged but did not reply. Of course they were bloody parasites, but why did he feel guilty about saying so? He thought back to the fire consuming his precious house, the roof collapsing in a shower of sparks. The column of flame roaring like a wild beast.

He had a strange feeling. An alarming feeling. He did not want to admit it, but he felt a sense of relief.

The ground was getting softer now. Soon they were walking through marshland, staggering under the weight of the bags as their feet slithered in the wet mud.

By nightfall both men were exhausted. They sat in silence in the growing darkness. Once again Goldman seemed ill at ease, but he did not risk saying anything about his fear.

'What's your name anyway?' asked the tramp. 'We've never been properly introduced.'

'What's it got to do with you?'

'I just thought it might be a bit more civilized if we knew each other's names.'

'Goldman,' he said reluctantly.

'Jewish?'

'I certainly am not. Church of England.'

He paused. 'What about you?'

'Jewish?' said the tramp. 'My family were – way back.'

'I meant your name, stupid.'

'Oh. Sheppard.'

There was silence. Then Goldman said, 'What made you think I was Jewish?'

'Well, Goldman sounds a bit – you know. I thought you might be . . .'

'Goldman's my business name. Chose it after a big finance outfit in the City. Sounds good. Strong. Inspires confidence. Respect.'

'Didn't they mind you using their name?'

'Who the hell cares? I can call myself what I like.'

'What's your real name, then?' asked Sheppard.

'That's none of your damn business,' snapped Goldman.

The hunter

The next morning they woke early but were too tired to move off straight away. Both men were in a pensive mood. Sheppard lay on his back on the grass, his hands clasped behind his head. Goldman sat close by, his knees drawn up and his arms locked round them as though holding himself in a safe place.

He thought back to the events of the previous day. The shock of finding Tresco abandoned and decaying. Then the fire. Why hadn't he been angry with Sheppard? Why hadn't he beaten the tramp to a bloody pulp?

It was strange – almost a betrayal of everything he stood for – but as he had watched the smoke and flames shooting up into the sky it was as though a weight was lifted from him. Not that he felt any pleasure at the release. Or at anything else. For one thing, there remained the nagging fear they were being followed. 'I still think there's something out there,' he said eventually. 'Watching us.'

'Relax,' said Sheppard, gazing up at the sky. 'It's your imagination.'

'I'm not so sure about that.'

'Listen,' said Sheppard. 'What you need to do is focus on something else. Think of happy times. Tell me about your life. What was going on in that big posh house of yours while I was sitting at the gate, waiting for my next encounter with Johnson? By the way,' he went on, 'did I ever tell you, Johnson wasn't very good at his job? He might have been an excellent butler, but he made a lousy thug. That beating he gave me on the last day? His heart wasn't in it. I hardly felt a thing. I think he was getting soft in his old age.'

'Why should I tell you anything?' demanded Goldman. 'It's got nothing to do with you.'

'I don't suppose it has,' said Sheppard. 'I was simply trying to make conversation. And maybe take your mind off this thing about being watched. You don't have to tell me anything if you don't want to.'

Goldman was silent. He stared into the distance. Why should he tell this stranger anything? Knowledge is power. The less people know about you the better.

On the other hand – what did it matter any more? What did anything matter? After what seemed a long time, he turned to Sheppard, who was still lying gazing up at the sky. 'OK, I'll tell you,' he said reluctantly. It felt as though some huge step had been taken, and he was not at all sure where it might be leading.

'That last year was good. Not just the money stuff. There were other things that made me realize I'd won. I was accepted. Against all the odds, I was one of the in-crowd. I was right there among the people who mattered.'

'Really?' said Sheppard.

'And you know what proved it? Two things.'

Sheppard sat up and looked across: 'Go on.'

'It was a couple of months ago. I got two phone calls. One was from the Dean's chaplain at the cathedral. He was ringing about the dedication of two new windows. One of them was mine. It had my company's name on it. Discreetly, at the bottom, of course. I'd donated a pile of money to the cathedral restoration. I remember the Dean coming on the line. He had real class. Very public school. Would I be able to join them at the dedication service and the reception afterwards? The Lord Lieutenant of the county would be there.'

The words were pouring out now. 'Think of it. There in stained glass for a thousand years: my name, my company. Me rubbing shoulders with old money. The landed gentry. Some of them were a bit sniffy about it – but screw the bastards, I say. What matters is that I'd made it.'

'So you fancied yourself as being part of the landed gentry, did you?' said Sheppard thoughtfully. 'I suppose that's what the butler thing was all about. I mean, who has butlers these days, for heaven's sake?'

'He came with the house,' replied Goldman, suddenly on his guard again.

'He did what?'

'He came with the house. I bought the house and all the stuff inside it. He was part of the deal.'

'Isn't that a bit unusual?'

'It was a takeover. The owners went bust and I bought them out.'

'Did they want to sell? I mean, weren't they quite fond of the old place?'

'Who cares about that? I played and won; winner takes all. They played and lost.'

'So you acquired Johnson along with the other fixtures and fittings: lock, stock and butler. Well, that explains how a nice guy like Johnson came to be working for someone like you.'

'I knew you'd sneer,' snapped Goldman.

'I wasn't sneering,' said Sheppard. 'But the butler thing does sound a bit odd. In fact, now I come to think about it, the whole thing sounds odd. The money, for instance. I can't quite see you giving money to a cathedral. In fact, it doesn't seem to be in your nature to give anything to anybody.'

'Who said anything about giving?' said Goldman. 'I wasn't giving, I was buying. Buying acceptance, respectability; buying credibility for my company. You can buy anything.'

'Even a butler,' said Sheppard, lying back and closing his eyes. He was smiling to himself as he thought about Johnson's fatherly concern – and the fiver he had offered him to go away. Away from danger. Johnson was a good man. 'So what was the other phone call about?' he asked.

'It was my tailor,' said Goldman. 'He was ringing to tell me my new riding outfit was ready.'

'You rode?' said Sheppard, sitting up again abruptly. 'You mean on a horse?'

'To hounds,' said Goldman.

'To hynds?' said Sheppard, mimicking an aristocratic accent. 'One rode to hynds, Golders? Well, good show. Jolly spiffing and all that.'

Goldman ignored the teasing. 'I was a member of the local hunt. It took a bit of getting into, but worth the effort. You should have seen it – a bloody great horse and me in my red coat with all the others. Lady this, the Honourable that, the Bishop of something or other. And yours truly.'

Sheppard lay back on the grass. 'Chasing foxes at the break of day is pretty top notch then?' he said, a hint of mischief in his voice.

'Brilliant sport,' said Goldman. 'Great exercise. Hammering along after the pack. The excitement of the chase. Dogs barking, horns blowing. It was wonderful.'

'Just like on the Christmas cards,' said Sheppard thoughtfully.

'Oh, come on,' said Goldman. 'You're just jealous.'

'I don't think I am,' said Sheppard, 'and I'm not sure the fox thought it was so wonderful either.'

'Stuff the fox,' retorted Goldman.

'Anyway, I thought that sort of thing was banned.'

'Think again,' said Goldman. 'Out in the country all sorts of things happen. It's tradition. A way of life.'

'That reminds me of a story I once heard about hunting,' said Sheppard, closing his eyes again.

Goldman was silent for a moment. 'Go on,' he said warily.

Sheppard gathered his thoughts, then said, 'There was once a rich young man who went hunting deer each morning with his hounds. One day, halfway through the chase, the young man was galloping through the woods when he came to a clearing. In the clearing was a lake where a young woman was bathing. She stepped out of the water just as the young man rode up. She was so beautiful he couldn't take his eyes off her.' He paused. 'Are you still listening?'

'Sure,' said Goldman. 'A guy on a horse surprises a chick with a gorgeous body and no clothes on. Of course I'm bloody listening.'

'OK,' said Sheppard. 'Except this young woman was a goddess and she was furious that a mere mortal had seen her naked. So, by magic, she turned him into a stag. The trouble was that, when the young man's hounds saw the stag, they did what they'd been trained to do and began to chase it. The man cried out to the dogs, but the hounds didn't recognize their master's voice.'

'And?'

'They tore the stag to death.'

There was a pause. Then Goldman said, 'That's a hell of a story. Did you make it up?'

'Not me. It's very old. Comes from the ancient Greeks, I think,' said Sheppard.

'Why did you tell it me?'

'Well, we were talking about hunting and it occurred to me you might be interested in seeing it from a different angle.'

'So you're into all that animal rights rubbish?'

'Not necessarily. It's just that ripping a living creature apart seems a very strange way of having fun. Also, you seem to be increasingly concerned that "something" out there is watching us. Maybe stalking us? So the subject of hunter and prey seems topical. Quite apart,' he added, 'from your business interests. And your sexual activities.'

Goldman was aware of an edge in Sheppard's voice. 'What about my business interests?' he demanded.

'Well,' said Sheppard, 'it's not for me to judge, but there does seem to be an element of the hunt in the way you seem to have gone after money. Pursued new opportunities without giving much thought to the people on the receiving end of your predatory enterprises. Takeover battles. Always making a killing. Sound familiar?'

'You're a bloody Commie.'

'Maybe I am, maybe I'm not. But at least the "bloody Commies" started out with good intentions. They often got it wrong, but they tried to do the right thing.'

There was a strained silence. 'Goldman,' said Sheppard at last.

'What?' said the other petulantly.

'No hard feelings?'

'Bollocks. You spoiled it,' said Goldman.

'What?'

'The memory of who I was – and what I did.'

'I'm sorry. Really – I am.'

'That's OK,' said Goldman cautiously, after a pause.

'But I bet you looked a sight in your Red Riding Hood outfit,' said Sheppard, and burst out laughing. He scrambled to his feet and ran off limping as Goldman reached for a stick to hurl at him.

Another man's shoes

It was cold. Flakes of snow danced ominously in the wind. 'All this walking is killing me,' complained Goldman. 'I'm frozen – my feet hurt and my shoulders ache.'

'We can't do anything about the weather or your feet, but you could try walking with your shoulders back,' said Sheppard. 'Keep your spine straight instead of stooping. Keep the weight over your hips, that might help.'

Goldman grimaced but said nothing. Later, though, he tried doing as Sheppard had suggested.

Eventually they stopped and put down their bags. The snow flurries had passed over but the wind was still raw. Goldman sat at the side of the road and took off his shoes. They were worn through. One had split, with the upper coming away from the sole.

'They've had it,' said Sheppard, wrinkling his nose at the smell. 'I'm surprised they lasted so long. We need to find you another pair. Some new socks as well.'

The cold air was damp now, as though it might rain.

'I don't recognize this place,' said Goldman. 'Where the hell are we?'

'Not sure,' said Sheppard.

Ahead of them, the land dropped away into a broad valley from where they could see, through the industrial haze, the lights of a city. Soon they joined a major road, heavy with traffic. It roared past, making their progress seem slower than ever. Along one side of the road was an area of untidy urban parkland and, in the distance, a wide concrete circle where an old bandstand had once stood. They walked over and sat on a bench. It was getting dark.

A couple of times Goldman glanced round as if someone had spoken to him.

'What is it?' asked Sheppard.

'I heard something. Someone's watching us,' said Goldman.

Sheppard sighed and was about to comment on Goldman's overactive imagination when there was a rustling in the bushes.

'Who's there?' yelled Goldman.

There was stillness. In the distance the traffic had thinned. A solitary car drove past the park. Then, silence. 'Who's there?' he shouted again, a note of fear in his voice.

There was more rustling in the bushes and a small man with ginger hair stumbled out into the half-light.

'What are you doing there?' said Goldman aggressively.

'Nothing. I wasn't doing nothing,' said the man, his face twitching nervously. He was pale and unshaven and his hair stuck up in tufts. He began to sidle away from them as if afraid. He had a wild look in his eyes, like an animal sensing danger.

'It's all right,' said Sheppard. 'We're not going to hurt you.'

The small man approached hesitantly. He stood in front of them, his hands trembling. His clothes were dirty and he smelt rancid and unwashed.

'Don't be afraid,' said Sheppard gently. 'My name's Sheppard and this is Goldman. We're looking for somewhere to doss down for the night.'

'Plenty of room here,' said the man, stammering nervously. 'In the bushes. Out of the way.' His head jerked. 'Where I sleep.'

'Do you always sleep here?'

The man nodded. 'In the bushes. Out of the way. Got an old sleeping bag.' His hands shook violently as if with the effort of talking.

'Is this really the best place?' asked Sheppard. 'Aren't there any hostels you could use?'

'Better here,' said the man. 'Away from people. In hostels you have to share a room. Very dangerous that is.'

'Dangerous?' said Goldman, surprised. 'Why?'

'Never know who the other person is. Maybe they hurt you. People on drugs. People with problems with their heads. Mental stuff. Frightens me. Safer to be here. Everybody knows that.'

'There are others?' said Goldman.

'A few. Mick and Taffy – and Gus. Gus is my mate.'

The man looked at Goldman and Sheppard more closely as his anxiety eased. 'Who are you, anyway?' he demanded. 'What you doing here?'

'We're travellers,' said Sheppard. 'Just bumming along. Like some of your pals.'

The man looked at their clothes suspiciously. He noticed Goldman's shoes. 'Maybe,' he said. 'You look like one of us, all right,' he said to Sheppard, 'but not him. He ain't one of us.' There was a moment's silence as though the man was coming to a decision. 'You eaten?' he said finally.

'No – not for a long time,' said Sheppard.

The man's head had stopped jerking and his hands had relaxed. He turned and disappeared back into the bushes, re-emerging a few moments later with a dirty white carrier bag. He pulled out some sandwiches, still in their plastic wrappings.

He caught Sheppard's enquiring look. 'Supermarket skip,' he said. 'Past their sell-by. But they're OK. We eat 'em all the time.'

The three sat and ate in silence. When they were finished, Sheppard brushed the crumbs off his jacket. 'Thanks,' he said. 'We don't even know your name.'

'Tommy,' said the man.

Sheppard nodded in greeting.

'How did you end up here?' asked Goldman.

Sheppard winced at the directness of the question, but Tommy did not seem to notice. He sat and stared across the park for some time, then said, 'I were in the Forces. Years back. Submarines. In the Falklands.' His head suddenly jerked again and his hands trembled. 'We sank her.'

'Sank what?' said Goldman.

'The *Belgrano*.'

'What?'

Tommy looked at him. 'A battleship. Old and slow. We caught her. Them Argies never had a chance. All them lads. We did that. We wasn't in any danger: they was running away. But we got them. "Gotcha", the papers said. Bastard papers.'

Sheppard looked thoughtful. 'And?' he said, gently probing.

'Can't forget. Started getting noises in me head. Couldn't sleep. Kept thinking of them lads in that old boat. Trapped in the hull, up ter their necks in water. Struggling ter get out. Crying for help. They was just lads. Lads with wives an' girlfriends, like us.' His head jerked again. 'Then I got discharged. Got nowhere to live, once I left. Started on the stuff. Never managed to settle.'

Then he got abruptly to his feet and stumbled off into the darkness without another word.

It started raining gently. There was no point in trying to light a fire. Instead Goldman and Sheppard sat under the trees. The branches, heavily leafed, spread a dark canopy over them keeping the rain off – at least for a time. Both men were deep in thought.

'He's weird,' said Goldman.

'He's had a rough time,' replied Sheppard.

'You think that stuff about the submarine really happened?'

'Who knows. Maybe it did – or perhaps it's all in his head.'

'Him and me both,' said Goldman bitterly.

'What do you mean?'

'Maybe this journey's all in my head. Some sort of bad dream. I mean, being here. We didn't come this way when we set off to find the house, so why is it different going back? It's crazy. It doesn't make any sense.'

'We're just following the path,' said Sheppard.

'Path? There is no damn path,' snapped Goldman. 'I haven't the foggiest idea where we're going – and I'm not sure you do either. It's pointless. A total waste of time.'

'Maybe there is a point to it,' said Sheppard. 'A purpose. Maybe something's happening, something really important. We just can't see what it is. But, judging by the pains in my back from sleeping on the ground, I'm pretty sure it's not a dream – bad or otherwise. When I wake up in the night with twigs sticking into me and wet grass tickling the back of my neck, it feels very real.'

'I thought you people didn't notice things like that,' said Goldman. 'I thought you'd be used to it.'

Sheppard glanced across at him but said nothing.

'So, where did you sleep, when you weren't squatting outside my house?' continued Goldman.

'All sorts of places. Derelict buildings, churchyards, rubbish skips. Anywhere there was cover. Places like this park sometimes.'

'It doesn't sound a bad life,' said Goldman reflectively. 'Out in the fresh air and all that.'

'In winter?' said Sheppard sharply. 'When you're cold, like we are now, or ill? When you see people driving past, their cars stuffed with food from the supermarket, going home to a warm bed and a wife or husband? OK, there were times when we were happy, and times when you can get by. But most of the lads lived in pain. That's why so many drink. Why they die so young. They can't compete with your world.'

'So it's my fault, is it?' demanded Goldman angrily.

'Yes, a lot of it is your fault. You and people like you,' said Sheppard. 'But now we're where they are. Out in the cold. Sleeping rough and wondering how it's going to end.'

Goldman was quiet for a long time, then said in a low voice, 'It's never going to end. Carrying my stuff, piece by piece. How can it end?'

'It's what you wanted.'

'Sheppard.'

'What?'

'Shut up and go to sleep.'

'Sure,' said Sheppard, 'but remember who's helping you carry your blasted bullion.'

There was no reply. In the darkness, the rain gently dripped down from the branches above.

* * *

The sound of traffic woke them the next morning. Stiff and cold, they were standing about unsure of what to do next when Tommy emerged sleepily from the bushes. 'Want some breakfast?' he asked. 'Take you down the centre if you like.'

'The city centre?' said Goldman.

'St Anne's,' said Tommy. 'Day centre. For lads like us. They do breakfasts.' He glanced down at Goldman's feet as though remembering. 'Clothes and shoes as well. Not always shoes; depends what they got in. Maybe you'll be lucky. Worth a try anyway.'

St Anne's was warm and crowded with people, the atmosphere heavy with cigarette smoke and unwashed bodies. A man sat sprawled at a table, fast asleep with his head on his arms. Across the room others sat, arguing or playing cards. Many had kept their coats on. 'Scared of losing them,' said Sheppard as he saw Goldman's puzzled expression. 'Their coats keep them warm in the night. Keep them alive.'

Josie, the young woman on reception, logged them in. 'You with Tommy?' she said. 'OK. Put your bags over there and help yourself to some food.' She turned to another woman. 'Is clothing open today?'

Josie turned back to Sheppard and Goldman and smiled. 'The clothing store opens at ten so you've got plenty of time to eat. The serving hatch is down there at the end of the room. Then it's upstairs for the clothes – you'll see the queue. Make sure you hang on to these tickets. They're so Peter knows to let you in. You can have one of everything. One shirt, one coat, one pair of shoes if they've got any to fit you. Plus socks and pants, if you need them.'

As they ate, Goldman realized he couldn't remember when he had last had a hot meal.

'Bacon, eggs, sausage, beans, fried bread. All loaded with lovely cholesterol,' said Sheppard, his lips coated in grease. 'Wonderful, wonderful grub.'

'I thought you were Jewish?' said Goldman accusingly.

45

Sheppard looked puzzled.

'The bacon?' said Goldman.

'Ah, well, not exactly. Jewish sympathies, perhaps.'

'Your mum wouldn't have approved.'

'I think she would. But you know the old saying: "In my father's house there are many menus."'

'Mansions,' said Goldman, 'many mansions.'

'Well, you're the expert on big houses,' said Sheppard, pushing back his chair and giving a quiet belch. 'Come on, let's see what they've got upstairs.'

'You can leave your stuff here while you go up,' Josie called from the reception desk.

Goldman looked alarmed. 'We'll take it with us,' he said, snatching up two of the bags.

Upstairs they queued with half a dozen other men in a gloomy corridor. Finally a young man opened a door at the end of the passage. 'Next please,' he called out.

'Why ain't there no bleedin' light in this corridor?' said one of the men. 'It ain't right making us queue up in the dark like this.'

'I'm sorry, mate,' said the young man. 'The bulb's bust. It's been like that for a couple of days. We've asked for someone to come and fix it.'

The clothing store was a long, narrow room with windows along one side that looked out across a railway line on to a disused factory. Racks of clothes on hangers filled the wall opposite the window. The room smelt of dust. An older man with an alarm button on a cord round his neck stood waiting as the small group of homeless men entered.

'Men's clothing at this end,' he called. 'Coats, jackets, shirts, pullovers. Trousers are in size order – please keep 'em that way. One of each and we need to book them out before you leave.'

The men spread out and started rummaging through the clothing. Goldman approached the older man. 'Are you Peter? They said downstairs that you might have some shoes.'

46

'You need to see my assistant over there,' said Peter cheerily. 'He's got a kind face. Don't know what kind, but there you are. Ha ha.' He laughed loudly at his own joke.

A man half-buried in a rack of coats turned and grimaced at Goldman. 'The gear's OK but the jokes are crap,' he said.

'Better that than the gear being crap, my son,' said Peter, overhearing the comment.

Goldman went over to the younger man. 'I need some shoes if you have any.'

'Eight and a halves?' he said, glancing down.

'How did you know what size I take?' asked Goldman.

'One of the few skills I've acquired in life,' the man replied, pulling a pair of black shoes out of a rack. 'You might just be lucky. We only got these in yesterday.'

Goldman sat down and took his old shoes off.

'You've walked a long way,' said the man, looking at the state of Goldman's feet.

Goldman tried the new shoes on and laced them up. Then he took a few tentative paces down the room.

'Any good?' asked Sheppard, coming over.

'Just about,' said Goldman, hesitating. 'Yes, I think they'll be OK.'

The young man was thoughtful for a moment. 'Do you know, the last person to wear those shoes was a bishop?'

Sheppard and Goldman looked unsure whether he was joking.

'Seriously. He died a few months ago and his widow sent his stuff. Those were his shoes. Good quality.'

'Well, they've come down in the world since then,' said Goldman.

'Oh, I'm not so sure about that,' said the younger man. 'I reckon old Stuart would be pleased that his shoes have gone to a good home. Some bishops seem to inhabit another world, but he was different.'

'You don't seem very keen on bishops,' said Sheppard.

The man gave him a hard look. 'Let's just say I don't find them the most inspiring of God's creatures,' he said.

'Are they all as bad?'

'Well, now you come to mention it, some of them have broken ranks recently. They started hammering the government over stuff like poverty and benefits. That took some guts, I admit. Especially when the press waded into the argument.'

'So what are you passionate about?' asked Sheppard.

The man hesitated, then indicated the older man further down the room. 'Same as him. Father Peter. Corny jokes, but a heart of gold. We don't see eye to eye on everything, but we do agree on respecting these lads and trying to find them decent shoes and coats. That and trying to make the world a better place. Love and justice.'

Sheppard smiled thoughtfully.

A man came up holding a pair of trousers. 'Peter says you can alter these,' he said. 'The legs are too long.'

'I can't do it now,' said the young man, 'but I'll sort them out when we close. If you wait in the canteen, I'll bring them down to you. Give me about an hour.'

Sheppard watched with amusement as the man walked away. 'I'll bet it's not often he comes across a bespoke tailoring service. How do you do it?'

'Adhesive tape,' said the man. 'Wonderful stuff. It irons on. You chop the trouser leg off and then turn the hem over. The tape melts with the heat of the iron and sets when it cools. Glues the hem up. Ten minutes and the job's done.'

'You're proud of that, aren't you?' said Sheppard.

'Too right I am,' said the man. 'Love your neighbour. I do it by shortening their legs.'

Sheppard chuckled.

'All right, lads. Time you were on your way,' Peter called from the other end of the room.

As they filed out, the younger man touched Sheppard on the sleeve. 'What happened to your wrists? You didn't –'

'No, I haven't been cutting myself,' said Sheppard, smiling. 'Just a bit of trouble with the law. A difference of opinion, you might say.'

The young man studied Sheppard thoughtfully. 'Have we met before?'

'Perhaps,' said Sheppard. 'And, who knows, we might meet again.'

'He's got a kind face,' Peter called down the room.

One of the homeless men groaned. 'All the old ones!'

'Pax vobiscum, Nil carborundum. Don't let the bastards grind you down,' Peter called back.

'He can't even speak decent Latin,' muttered the homeless man.

Out on the street Sheppard and Goldman checked the bags of coins. A man full of drink stood shouting incoherently in the entrance to the day centre. His face was a fiery red, his eyes wild and unfocused.

Goldman turned to Sheppard but he shook his head. 'It's no use. There's nothing we can do. Time to move on.'

Meanwhile Tommy had joined them on the street. 'You lads OK?'

'I've got a pair of shoes and some socks,' said Goldman, grudgingly. 'And some sandwiches they gave us for later.'

'That's thanks to you, Tommy,' said Sheppard. 'We owe you. Take care and I hope your head gets better. I'm sure those men on the old battleship wouldn't want to see a fellow sailor suffering. Anyway, what happened wasn't your decision. That rests with someone else. Remember that.'

Tommy held out a trembling hand. 'Thank you. Them's kind words. Maybe I will put it behind me, like you say. I'll try, anyway. And you won't forget me, will you?' he added, a note of desperation in his voice. 'Please don't forget me.'

'We won't,' said Sheppard.

'And I won't forget you neither,' said the small man.

He glanced at Goldman. 'Nor you, guv'nor.' He paused. 'You've been good pals. Treated me proper. I'm going to miss yer.' His hands were shaking badly now and he seemed close to tears. 'I could do with a smoke. Don't suppose you got a fag?' he added hesitantly.

Goldman felt the irritation rise up inside him. Always on the scrounge, these people. All the bloody same. On the other hand, he thought, he did have a new pair of shoes. He frowned, as though struggling to make up his mind about something. Then he produced from his pocket the pack of cigarettes he had taken from his driver, Henshaw. Reluctantly, he took one out and passed it to Tommy.

'Thanks, guv'nor,' said Tommy, grinning with relief.

Goldman seemed to be in pain. 'Take the pack,' he growled through clenched teeth, as though unable to get the words out clearly.

'Cor, thanks, mister,' said Tommy, opening the pack to see how many cigarettes it contained. 'Almost full. Thanks a lot.'

'I didn't know you smoked,' said Sheppard.

'I don't,' snapped Goldman.

As they walked away they saw a woman sitting in a doorway begging. Beside her was a small boy. He looked pale. Probably drugs, thought Goldman. In the child's hand was a scrap of blue rag.

Sheppard stopped and said something to the woman. She smiled. Then he squatted down beside her and gave her the sandwiches.

Goldman said nothing and walked on. Something stirred in his memory. Something from long ago that brought back an aching pain. A scrap of blue rag . . . was he dreaming? Maybe he was going mad. He was certainly confused – and angry with himself.

He thought about Tommy. Why did I give him those damn cigarettes? You never give anything away. Never. That's the way you succeed in life. Give nothing. Ever. And anyway, what the hell am I doing here? Where are we going? What's happening to me? He felt like a child, frightened and alone in a strange city. He wanted to cry. He stopped and looked back to make sure Sheppard was still there.

Moments later Sheppard caught up with him and his fear subsided. Goldman straightened his tie and carried on walking on as though nothing had happened.

Part 2

The sea

Stumbling and staggering over rough ground, they pressed on. They walked for days, until the busy city was far behind them. The atmosphere was different now. Goldman noticed that the air smelt fresher and there was a distinct breeze. He stopped and looked up at the cloudless sky.

'What is it?' said Sheppard.

'Not sure. Something feels different. And that bird: it's circling as though it's searching for something. Looks like a seagull.'

As they struggled up yet another hill, the dead weight of the bags dragged painfully on their shoulders and arms. 'Nearly at the top,' grunted Sheppard. 'Then we can take a break.'

Emerging from the trees, they stopped in amazement. They dropped the bags of money and stood speechless. Below, stretching out into the glare of the reflected sun, was a vast expanse of sea. 'Bloody hell,' said Goldman.

'Something like that,' said Sheppard thoughtfully. 'I have to admit I wasn't expecting this. Come on, let's go and see where the path goes.'

After the long march, the clear blue of the sea filled both men with a childlike delight. The path dropped away steeply and they had to concentrate on where they were putting their feet to avoid stumbling.

As they reached the beach they found themselves at the edge of a wide, curving bay. In the distance an elderly man and a much younger woman were sitting by a sunshade. The woman, probably in her early thirties, was wearing a blue and white striped T-shirt and a pair of white shorts. Laughter drifted across the sand. Nearby a sailing boat was moored to a simple wooden jetty, the boat rocking gently with the movement of the water.

'This sure as hell isn't the way we came,' muttered Goldman.

'Never mind that. Let's see if they can tell us where we are,' said Sheppard.

As they made their way across the beach their feet sank into the powdery sand, making the walking even more laborious. The man and woman looked up and waved.

'Greetings,' said the man amiably. His grey hair, like his jeans, was thin and faded. 'Come far?'

'We seem to have been walking for ever,' said Goldman.

The old man smiled. 'They all say that.'

'All?' said Goldman.

'We get plenty passing this way. A bit of a quiet spell at the moment. Anyway, sit down and have something to eat. It's only bread and cheese, but better than nothing.' He glanced across at the young woman. 'This is Rosie – she runs the boat with me. Partners, you might say.'

Rosie raised a hand in greeting and smiled. Fabulous legs, thought Goldman, his mind going back to Trudi. And the rest looks pretty damn good, too.

When they had finished eating, Goldman and Sheppard sat back and began to relax in the warmth of the sun. Goldman said, 'What did you mean about people passing through?'

It was Rosie who answered. 'We get a lot of people coming over the hills following the path. Usually they bring more stuff than you. Is this all you've got?'

'It's enough,' said Goldman. 'It's pulling my arms out of their sockets.'

'Metal,' said Sheppard. 'And heavy.'

'Ah, heavy metal,' said the old man closing his eyes for a moment. 'Great music.'

'Stop it,' laughed Rosie, throwing a handful of sand in his direction. 'This is serious.'

'So were the bands,' said the old man. 'That was serious music.'

'Still is,' said Sheppard. 'But we need to be moving. Where does the path go from here? We're heading for the river . . .'

'We know where you're heading,' said the old man. His voice blended with the lapping of the waves in the shingle. 'But there's no path. Not one you can see, anyway.'

'So what happens now?' asked Goldman with anxiety in his voice.

'You need to get over there,' said the man, pointing directly out to sea. 'You'll probably pick up the path on the other side.'

'Probably? What do you mean by that? Is there a path or isn't there?' said Goldman. 'And where is it? I can't see anything that looks like the other side.'

Rosie laughed. 'Trust us, it's there. You just have to set off. We've done it lots of times.'

'And you'd better be going,' said the old man. 'There's not many hours of daylight left.'

'Aren't you coming with us?' asked Sheppard.

'No, Rosie can take you. She's handy with a boat. You'll be fine with her.'

Goldman was about to speak but Sheppard's frown silenced him. Together they carried their bags along the wooden jetty and stowed them in the hull of the sailing boat. Rosie jumped in after them and cast off the moorings. Then, hauling on the main sheet, she began to raise the large white sail.

'Doesn't this thing have an engine?' said Goldman in alarm.

'No – we've never needed one. Anyway, the wind's with us today, and freshening, so it should be a brisk passage.'

Goldman sat near the bags of money, clutching himself with his arms, uneasy at the word 'brisk' and the thought of being without an engine. He was silent for a long time. Rosie sat in the stern with one hand on the tiller, though the boat seemed to need little by way of steering.

'Are you OK?' said Sheppard, after an hour or so.

'No,' said Goldman. 'I hate water. And I hate being in a boat.'

'What is there to hate?' said Sheppard. 'A nice trip in the sun with a good-looking young woman taking care of us.'

'I don't like being out of my depth, that's what.'

'Well, you're certainly out of your depth here,' Rosie called from the stern. She was sitting with her eyes closed, enjoying the sun on her tanned skin.

'Meaning what?' said Goldman.

'We're into deep water out here, that's all.'

'Deep? How deep?' demanded Goldman.

'I'm not sure,' she called back, her eyes still closed. 'The beach slopes gradually and then shelves away steeply. I'd say a good few hundred fathoms.'

'That's impossible. Are you saying this water's half a mile deep?'

'Who knows,' said Rosie lazily. 'Half a mile – a mile – who's counting?' She was smiling, her face still lifted to the sun. She began to sing very quietly to herself.

'Turn back,' shouted Goldman, panicking. 'Please go back. I want to get off. I can't do this.'

Sheppard took his arm, but Goldman pulled away angrily.

'You're quite safe,' said Rosie, wide awake as if something was about to happen. 'Look, even if you fell overboard, you wouldn't sink.'

'Of course you would,' shouted Goldman. 'That's why people drown. They drown in the sea all the time.'

'But I'm not sure this is the sort of sea you're used to,' said Rosie. 'You can't sink in this water. Must be the specific gravity. Too much salt. Try jumping in.' She smiled. 'In fact, now I think about it, you could both do with a wash. I don't want to be personal but neither of you smells very wonderful right now. Don't worry – I'll wait for you,' she added cheerily.

'That's a good idea,' said Sheppard with a grin. 'I can't remember when I last had a wash – or him, come to that.'

'No way!' snapped Goldman. 'No way am I getting into that water.'

'Listen,' said Sheppard. 'Have I ever let you down? You know what they say: confront the thing that scares you. Face your demons. Rosie says you'll float. It could even be fun.'

'To hell with that. I'm not doing it,' shouted Goldman desperately.

'I think you are,' said Sheppard. He turned towards the girl. 'Rosie?'

The young woman pulled the rope controlling the mainsail out of the cleat that was holding it taut. She pushed the tiller over and the bow swung round into the wind until the little craft lay still in the water.

The boat rocked as Rosie and Sheppard advanced on Goldman like two sheepdogs cornering a reluctant ram.

'No!' yelled Goldman.

'Yes!' cried Sheppard and Rosie as they heaved Goldman over the side.

There was a huge splash as he hit the water and started threshing the surface with his arms. Rosie watched for a moment and then turned to Sheppard. 'That's very odd. He's sinking.'

'Oh no,' muttered Sheppard, pulling off his shoes. 'Don't go without us,' he called as he leapt over the side.

'I wouldn't dream of it,' Rosie muttered to herself as she looked down at the two men in the water.

'Can't you swim?' Sheppard shouted to Goldman.

The other man, struggling desperately to stay afloat, seemed not to hear the question as the fear engulfed him. Sheppard swam across and grabbed him by the jacket. 'I've got you. Stop struggling,' he yelled.

'Sinking,' shrieked Goldman. 'Don't let me go down there.'

Sheppard had a thought. 'Your pockets! What have you got in your pockets?' he shouted.

The question seemed to increase Goldman's panic.

'What's in your blasted pockets?' Sheppard repeated, realizing that they were both in danger of being dragged down. For a second he contemplated the mile of green emptiness beneath them.

'Some of the money,' shouted Goldman.

'Empty your pockets. Now. Get rid of it before we both go down.'

A small wave lapped against Sheppard's face and he choked as the salt water went down his throat.

'It's my stuff. It's mine!' shouted Goldman.

'Stuff your bloody stuff,' retorted Sheppard, coughing to try to clear his throat and struggling to support Goldman. 'Lose it, or go down. It's your choice.'

Goldman fumbled with his jacket pockets as Sheppard fought to keep their heads above water. The coins were falling as though in slow motion through the green water like autumn leaves. More golden discs followed.

Goldman was lighter in Sheppard's arms. He was floating. Finally he stopped struggling and Sheppard let go. They were both being buoyed up by the water.

'Are you OK now?' asked Sheppard.

'Sort of,' said Goldman, unsure of the new sensation of floating.

Sheppard turned to where the boat was rocking gently in the water. 'Rosie?' he called. Her head appeared over the side.

'Permission to come aboard?'

'Are you clean?'

'Inside and out!' yelled Sheppard.

Despite the water in their clothes, Rosie pulled the two men back into the boat with surprising ease. Goldman realized that she was a lot stronger than she looked.

'That's better,' she said brightly. 'I don't want smelly boys on my boat.'

Goldman scowled sullenly at the teasing. It was some minutes before he was willing to talk.

'Now, let's see what we've got here,' said Rosie when Goldman had stopped frowning. She pulled an old biscuit tin from under one of the seats. 'Goldman, you can have a piece of cake for being brave.'

'Brave? Him? What about me?' protested Sheppard. 'It was me that jumped in and rescued him when he was sinking.'

'Yes, you did. You were a good Sheppard, and you may have some cake too.' Rosie pulled the main rope tight again and snagged it in the cleat. The big white sail filled contentedly, as though the boat had been waiting to continue on its way. The three sat eating cake and enjoying the warmth of the sun.

'This is OK,' said Goldman tentatively, after a while.

'The cake?' said Sheppard.

'Being here.'

'But you hate water and boats?'

'I know, but I feel better about that now. A bit better.'

'Well, don't get too comfortable,' said Rosie, getting to her feet. 'Things could be about to get interesting.'

The storm

Rosie was standing in the stern looking intently at a cloud formation far ahead of them.

'What is it?' said Goldman, looking anxious.

'Big weather.'

'A storm?' said Sheppard.

Rosie was silent for a moment. 'Might be. And we're heading right for it. Things may get a bit bumpy for a while, but don't worry.'

'Sheppard.' Goldman was tugging at Sheppard's sleeve. His eyes were fixed on the approaching clouds, staring as if hypnotized by the dark mass. 'Sheppard,' he said urgently.

'What?' said Sheppard. 'Stop pulling my sleeve.'

'It's happening again,' said Goldman.

Sheppard turned to him. 'What is? What are you talking about?'

'In the night. In the woods. I told you. Something watching. Something predatory. It feels the same now. Oh God, Sheppard, I can't do this stuff.' Goldman sank to his knees in the bottom of the boat and started to cry.

'What do we do?' said Sheppard as Rosie began to reduce sail.

'Batten down the hatches and brace yourselves.'

'There aren't any hatches,' said Sheppard.

Rosie gave him a long look over her shoulder as she sheeted in the mainsail and lashed it in neat folds along the horizontal wooden boom. 'I know,' she said. 'Tie a length of line round you and Goldman. Then lash yourselves to the boat. If anyone goes over the side, we don't want to lose them.'

'Are you scared?' said Sheppard.

'Well, I'm not exactly dancing a jig,' said Rosie tartly. 'But at least we won't sink if we go overboard.'

The wind was gripping the boat now. Huge waves exploded against the bow, sluicing gallons of water into the open craft. Goldman was lying on the floor in a foetal position, his hands over his face.

Then the full fury of the gale was upon them. The boat seemed to be alive as it pitched high out of the water, then slammed back with shuddering force as each wave hammered into it. Sheppard glanced across at Rosie through the sheeting rain. Her face was pale, but there was no panic in her eyes as she fought to keep the bow heading into the storm.

Goldman was being thrown violently about in the well of the boat as each wave smashed into the small craft. The boat seemed to corkscrew, hurling him against the planking, lifting him up and then dashing him down again. One moment his face was in the water that was flooding the boat, the next he could see the sky, purple and malevolent above him, as though some immense creature was intent on devouring him. He screamed out for help, but his shrieks were snatched away in the howling gale.

Sheppard was suddenly aware of Rosie calling to him. 'Bail. Under the seat. The cake tin. Bail the water out.'

How long the storm lasted, they had no idea. It seemed an eternity until the clouds passed and the sky lightened. Finally there was peace.

* * *

Goldman stirred in the bottom of the boat. Rosie appeared to be asleep at the tiller, her head dropped forward on her chest. The gale had dropped to a fresh breeze. Goldman sat up slowly. 'Are we still in one piece?'

Rosie opened her eyes, squinting in the sunlight. 'Just about.'

'Any cake left?' asked Goldman.

'Sorry. We had to use the tin to get the water out of the boat. The last bit of cake went over the side hours ago. Maybe days ago,' she added, rubbing her back.

'That was a very strange storm,' said Sheppard.

Goldman looked at Sheppard but said nothing. There would be plenty of time to talk later.

The rest of the voyage was peaceful. Goldman was almost enjoying himself. There was something therapeutic about the movement of the boat and the warmth of the sun on his skin. He glanced back at Rosie sitting at the tiller. She was intent on the progress of the boat and was singing quietly.

Suddenly she shaded her eyes against the sun. 'Almost there,' she said.

Goldman stood up, holding firmly to the mast with both hands. In the distance he could see white surf against the shore. Out in open water there had been little sensation of speed, but as they got closer to land Goldman realized they were moving fast. Running parallel with the shoreline, he could see breakers crashing against the rocks, throwing plumes of spray high into the air.

'Hold tight,' shouted Rosie, and put the tiller hard over. The boat turned abruptly so that it was now on a broad reach, heading straight for the breakers. Both men shouted in alarm as the rocks rushed towards them. But at the last moment Rosie eased the tiller a fraction and the little boat shot through a gap in a shower of spray. Goldman could have reached out and touched the massive rocks that leapt up, dark and threatening, on both sides of the boat.

A wave carried them forward into calmer water and the boat grounded firmly on a shingle beach. The two men were speechless, shocked into silence.

'Is there a problem?' asked Rosie.

'Not now,' said Sheppard. Goldman said nothing.

'Are you OK?' she asked Goldman.

'I was scared. I thought we were done for.'

Rosie smiled. 'You needn't have worried. We haven't lost a passenger yet.'

Getting out of the boat was more difficult than getting in. There was no jetty and their feet sank in the shingle as they stepped over the side into the warm, shallow water.

Goldman noticed that the young woman's bare legs were brown against her white shorts. He remembered his young sister's suntanned feet and legs as she splashed in the waves on one of their rare family holidays.

They lifted the heavy bags out of the boat and staggered up the beach.

'Go well,' said Rosie. 'I hope you've dried out by now.'

'Thanks,' said Sheppard. 'It's been good to see you.'

Goldman realized that Sheppard and the young woman had the same look about them, as though they might be brother and sister.

Rosie held out her hand to Goldman. 'Until we meet again,' she said. Her handshake was surprisingly firm. She turned to Sheppard. 'Watch how you go.' She opened her arms and kissed him lightly on both cheeks, then gently pushed him away. 'Get going, you two. You've got a long journey ahead of you.'

'I don't want to go,' said Goldman. He paused. He wanted to hug her but was somehow afraid. Anyway, he thought, when had he ever wanted to hug anyone? Hug them with real love and affection? His mother and his younger sister, perhaps. But that had been in the good days, before the darkness came. After that there had been nobody, not even Trudi. Not until now.

'Out there – you kept us safe,' he stammered. 'You've been great. Wonderful.'

Rosie grinned. 'You slept through most of it. But you've learned to swim, so it's not all been wasted.'

Sheppard was thoughtful. 'This may not be goodbye, anyway. We could be passing this way again in the future. Quite a few times. There's a lot more stuff back there.'

Goldman's smile disappeared at the thought of the ruins of what had been Tresco. And all his other possessions. He shivered.

'Come on, boys,' said Rosie crisply, realizing that Goldman was beginning to sink back into despair. 'Let's get this trip over with first.' She glanced up the beach. 'That looks like the path over there.'

They picked up their bags once more and set out for the tree-covered hills that fringed the bay. They had not gone more than a few yards before Rosie called out. 'Goldman!'

He turned and saw that she was beckoning to him. He walked back and stopped. She was frowning.

'What?' he asked uncertainly.

'Hug?' she said.

'I though you were cross with me.'

'I was teasing,' she said with a smile.

* * *

They walked for some time before stopping to look back. The boat was far out on the water, travelling fast in the freshening wind. Spray burst from the bow as it rode the waves. For a moment they could see the tiny figure of Rosie in the stern; then the boat was lost in the reflection of the evening sun on the water.

As they moved off again, Goldman said, 'You know her, don't you? From before, I mean.'

'Sort of,' said Sheppard.

'She's quite a woman – young but wise at the same time.'

'A good person to know,' agreed Sheppard, gasping for breath as he climbed the steep path.

'Do you think she'll get back before nightfall?' said Goldman.

'Do you care?'

'No, of course not.' He paused. 'Not really. Well, yes. A bit.'

'You've changed your tune,' said Sheppard. 'That swim seems to have done you good. Maybe we should have let you splash round out there a bit longer.'

'Bollocks. That's all in your imagination. I haven't changed,' said Goldman.

Sheppard smiled but said nothing.

The two continued up the hillside and into the dark canopy of trees. Sheppard looked across at Goldman. 'What is it?'

'Nothing. I was just thinking about Rosie,' said Goldman.

The lost boy

They lay in the darkness, each aware that the other was awake. The night was still and warm. There had been no need for the fire but they had lit it anyway. Henshaw's cigarette lighter was earning its keep.

Though neither spoke of it, they were both missing the companionship of the boat crossing. Now the dying embers of the fire glowed comfortingly in the dark.

'Goldman?'

'Yes?'

'You OK?'

'Yes. I was just thinking. I've never really looked at the sky. At the stars. There's a lot of them. They're brighter than I thought. Almost as though they're alive.'

There was a silence, then Sheppard said, 'Can I ask you something? About money. All the stuff you've done. What was it all about? What makes you – made you – do it?'

Goldman was quiet for a long time, as though trying to make up his mind about something important. 'Maybe it was about showing people I was better than they were,' he said. 'Proving that I could be the best. It made me feel good. Powerful. It gave me a buzz that I could out-think and out-manoeuvre the others. See an opportunity and move in fast – move in first. Exploit it, like it was a game. A game I could win.' He paused. 'Anyway, there was nothing else. Nothing that mattered.'

'So why did you need to prove that you were better than the others?' asked Sheppard. 'Does it matter who's best?'

'Listen, you don't know what it's like coming from a useless family; being a kid in the gutter. Your dad coming home and beating the hell out of you because he's been laid off at the pit and spent the week looking for another job. Selling stuff from the house to get more money for drink, till there's hardly a chair to sit on.'

'Was it always like that?' asked Sheppard.

'No. Only later. In the early days he grew roses. He had a beautiful little garden then. Everything planted in neat rows. Beans, cabbages, tomatoes. He had time for us. Took us for walks. We had caravan holidays at the sea. It always seemed to be sunny. We were warm – safe. Then one day it all changed.'

'What happened?'

'The pit had shut. When I came home from school that day, the garden looked as though a bomb had hit it. All the plants had been torn up and the roses trampled into the mud. He'd gone mad. Mad with drink. Mad with pain. He'd destroyed his own garden, just like he'd been destroyed. Weeds began to grow where there had been flowers and rows of vegetables. Dogs came in and crapped all over the place, till there was nothing but shit and nettles.'

'Did no one try to help?'

'Our friends and neighbours tried to cheer him up, but it was hopeless. All he seemed interested in was drinking himself senseless – that and his fags. God, I used to hate those bloody cigarettes. The whole house stank of them. Eventually everyone gave up. Turned their backs on us. What else could they do? That was when the nightmare started – and it went on for years. My mum and my sister seemed to lose the will to live; but I didn't.'

'So what did you do?'

'I fought. When you're a kid in that situation you either lie down and die or you stand up and fight. I fought for every penny I possess. I showed my dad that I was better than he was. Better than all of them. Nobody was going to beat me any more. I was safe.'

'And that's it? All of it?' said Sheppard.

Goldman was silent. Finally he said, 'Maybe there was something else. The world's a big place and it's easy to feel you don't matter. Look at those stars – millions of them. Been there for millions of years, and they'll be there for millions more years. And what are we?

Here today and gone tomorrow. But I wanted to be noticed. To be significant. To have power. To climb out of the gutter and be someone. And I was, Sheppard. I was someone.'

'Who were you?' asked Sheppard, his voice coming out of the night. The fire had died now but the breeze was warm.

'Someone whose word really meant something. Someone people looked up to. Obeyed. Depended on. Admired. Feared.'

'Is that what you wanted? To be feared?'

'It's better than being ignored,' snapped Goldman bitterly. 'Better than being walked over. Beaten up.'

'Tell me about it,' muttered Sheppard, remembering his last encounter with Johnson and other, more dramatic, events in his life. 'So you did that to other people? Walked over them? Beat them up?'

'Sometimes. But at least I gave them work. Created wealth and jobs. Built a business that stretched across the world. From the gutter I did that. On my own. I got a new name. A new life. It was thrilling to be on top. And I was on top. I never had much in the way of toys as a kid, but I sure as hell made up for it later. I had my own private jet with my own pilot to fly it. And, boy, did that thing go. I was up there in the clouds and nobody could touch me. I was never going to be afraid again.'

'And weren't you afraid after that?'

There was silence. Goldman looked up at the stars through the tree branches. He realized that they were moving very slowly across the night sky. 'Yes,' he said quietly. 'I was always afraid. No matter what I did or how much I got, I was still scared. Scared of losing it all. Scared of the big man coming home and hitting me with his leather belt. Scared of being a nobody.'

'And wasn't there anyone who loved you, who believed in you?' said Sheppard in the darkness.

'My sister and my mum. They did. For a while.'

'And then what?'

'My mum died. It was sudden. She was taken ill in the night. It was her appendix. I remember the ambulance men carrying her out of the house on a stretcher. She never opened her eyes. She never said goodbye.'

'What about your sister?'

She was younger than me. Her and Mum were close – very much alike. She never got over it. Went a bit mental. She started mixing with a bad crowd. Doing drugs. Trying to find somewhere to belong, I suppose. She ended up on the streets and we lost touch. I should have looked after her better.'

'And was that it? No one else?' said Sheppard.

Goldman was silent for a moment, then said, 'There was a kid at school. A boy called Jonathan. One of your lot. Jewish. Good family. Caring family. They'd been refugees way back, but there was always warmth and laughter at their house. And nice food. They made me feel wanted. He was my friend, Jonathan. My best friend.'

'So what happened to him?'

'They moved away. Went to live down south. We lost touch.'

'You never saw him again?'

'No.'

'What was Jonathan's other name?'

'Why do you ask?'

'No particular reason.'

'They were called Goldman.'

'So you took his name?'

'Yes, in a way.'

'What was that about?'

'I don't know. A way of being with him, I suppose. Not losing him completely. Wanting to be part of his family. Wanting to belong.'

'But you said you chose your name because of some big-shot firm in the City.'

'That was a coincidence. It fitted somehow.'

'And it made a difference?'

'Not really. Like I said, after they were gone, there was no one. I got married once but it didn't work. She was American. She went back to her mum. I made up my mind then that I would never need another person again. I'd be safer on my own.'

'And were you?'

'I thought I was. With all the deals I did and all the money I made. But underneath, deep down, nothing changed. Look at a rich man, Sheppard, and what do you see? Money? Power? But what's really there? Nothing but a frightened child, lost in the world.'

'A lost little boy? That doesn't sound much like you,' said Sheppard.

'Me? I don't even know who I am any more.'

There was silence. Then Sheppard spoke again. 'Are you afraid now?'

'Yes, a bit. How can you not be, out here in the dark with something prowling round out there in the woods? Not knowing what the hell's happening or where we're going. But not afraid in the same way. Not the sort of fear that overwhelms you. At least I've got you to talk to in the night. You are still awake, aren't you?'

'Wide awake,' said Sheppard.

'You should have been a shrink,' said Goldman. 'You're good at listening.'

'Do I have a choice?'

Goldman laughed. It was a sound Sheppard had not heard before.

Then Goldman said, 'I wasn't afraid of dying, you know. I was afraid of disappearing. Of being invisible. That's worse than dying. Maybe that's why people do such terrible things. Kill other people. Start wars. Jump off the tops of buildings. Anything to be noticed. To be visible, even for a moment.' He paused. 'Hurting people's a good way to do that. Fly a plane into a skyscraper and everybody notices. Do a kind deed and nobody sees. So you steal and grab and bully and shout. You make sure every other bastard knows you're there. That you're important, and anyone who doesn't agree with that is going to get hurt.'

'So at the end of the day, who does notice you?' said Sheppard. 'Apart from Raffa, back at the river with his straw hat and his clipboard?'

'And you,' said Goldman. 'You notice me.' He was quiet. Then he said, 'That's really funny. You're the scruffy tramp I kept sending Johnson to chase away. You were nothing, and yet it ends up you're all I've got. Why didn't you pack it in and sit outside someone else's front gate?'

Sheppard thought for a moment. 'Maybe I was trying to warn you.'

'About what?'

'All this,' said Sheppard. 'Trying to tell you what might be heading down the tracks, coming your way. Hoping things could be different, perhaps.'

'Are you saying that you knew all this crap was going to happen?' said Goldman.

'I had a sneaking feeling.'

Goldman turned to where Sheppard was lying in the darkness. 'Who the hell are you?' he said.

'Like you said, I'm a tramp – a parasite.'

'But before that? In the beginning?'

Sheppard shrugged. 'In the beginning? Oh, a bit of this, a bit of that.'

'Doing what?' demanded Goldman.

Sheppard sighed. 'OK, if you really want to know, I was a scribe. Newspaper work. Writing.'

'You were a journo?'

'For a while. Makes begging sound respectable, doesn't it?'

'Were you any good at it?'

'Yes – as a matter of fact I was. And I worked with some great people. There was one guy called Anderson. He was brilliant. Taught me a hell of a lot.'

'So why did you jack it in?' asked Goldman. 'I mean, it sounds a damn sight more fun than sleeping rough.'

'I got fired.'

'For stealing?'

Sheppard chuckled. 'Worse than that. I got sacked for arguing.'

'You're kidding.'

'Nope. It was during the miners' strike. Some of us in the union got fed up with the politics of the paper. The government was trying to break the miners and the paper was backing the government. Some of us were very unhappy about that and said so.'

'Weren't you tempted just to toe the line – do as you were told?'

'Yes, we were all tempted in our different ways.'

'Then what happened?'

'The pits were shut, we got the push – and the paper got bought out by some big conglomerate.'

Goldman was silent for a time. Then he said, 'That's a load of bullshit.'

'What is?'

'That stuff about working for a paper in the miners' strike. I was seven years old when all that happened. My dad was one of the men who got laid off. That was forty years ago. You'd be well into your sixties by now.'

'I look young for my age,' said Sheppard. 'It's all this fresh air and exercise I'm getting.'

'Seriously, you idiot, tell me,' insisted Goldman.

Sheppard groaned in exasperation. 'Questions, questions! I'll tell you some other time. Right now you're keeping me from my beauty sleep.'

Goldman laughed. It was a gentle, companionable laugh.

'Yeah, get some sleep,' he said. 'Tomorrow is another day. Maybe another bloody world.'

'What do you mean by that?' said Sheppard quietly.

'I don't know quite. Ever since we got off Rosie's boat it's been different. As though we're in a different place: a different part of the world. It's like we're being taken somewhere. Led. How the hell do I know, Sheppard? I don't know anything any more. Sheppard?'

But there was only the sound of quiet snoring.

Goldman lay awake for a long time, his mind in turmoil. Why did I tell him all that stuff about myself? he wondered. I broke the rule: tell people nothing. Knowledge is power. Give people power and they destroy you.

Is that Sheppard's game? No, he doesn't seem to play games. He's different, and yet – there's something familiar about him. As though we've met somewhere before. Goldman remembered having that same thought back at Tresco as Sheppard stood watching him put the money into the bags.

Suddenly, it came to him. He reminds me of Jonathan. In the darkness Goldman smiled.

The wonderful day

Many miles away, Ahmed Hussein opened his eyes. He lay still, listening to the silence of the house. Beside him in the half-light of dawn, his young wife stirred in her sleep and moaned quietly. The gripping pains of childbirth were stronger now. The contractions were coming more regularly.

Ahmed lay waiting. This was the wonderful day. The day of their firstborn. Please God that it should be a boy. Please God that it should be healthy, he thought. Please God that Rosmira should be safely delivered of this child.

Suddenly the young woman woke with a cry. 'It's happening. It has started.'

'Is everything well?'

'No; I am not sure,' she said. She felt under the bed covering and laughed. 'My waters, they have broken. Please fetch the woman. Hurry. Go now!'

Ahmed scrambled out of bed. He pulled on a pair of ragged trousers, running barefoot into the dust of the street, still struggling to pull up the zip and tuck in his shirt. It was the curfew, but still he ran. Into the next street. Which house? There were no numbers. This one? No – it was this one. He knocked urgently on the shabby door, its blue paint peeling from neglect and poverty.

He knocked again. Eventually a large, elderly woman appeared. 'Is it now?' she asked calmly.

'Yes. Come quickly. Please come quickly.'

'There is no need to rush, my son,' she said, picking up an old shopping bag. 'The little one will wait a few more minutes.' She sighed. 'You men: you are all the same. Rushing here, rushing there. Now, let us go quietly unless you want to be shot by the soldiers for breaking the curfew and have your child born to a grieving widow.'

They walked down the street and back to the house where Rosmira was lying on the bed, groaning.

'Be still, my daughter,' said the older woman. 'Let it take its own time.' She turned to the hovering shadow that was Ahmed. 'You: go and make yourself useful. Fetch some hot water. And don't look so worried. These things have happened before.'

Gradually the day unfolded into light. The sky was clear blue and it would once again be hot. Very hot. Inside the house the women waited and Ahmed fretted. Gradually the labour pains became more frequent and Rosmira cried out. 'Leave us now,' said the old woman to Ahmed. 'This is work for women, not men.'

In the next room Ahmed waited. Two neighbours came in to join him in his vigil. The long wait continued into the afternoon and Ahmed's anxiety increased with each passing hour.

'It will be well,' said one of the neighbours solicitously. 'These things cannot be hurried. I remember when my daughter was having her first child she –'

The door to the bedroom opened abruptly. The old woman came out with a worried look on her face.

'Is it well?' said Ahmed anxiously. 'Is it not born yet?'

'Your wife is well,' said the woman. 'But she is becoming exhausted. The baby still does not come and I am not sure why. We need to get her to a hospital. It is not serious but we have to go now. They will have the equipment we need. Do not worry.'

'But how can we get to the hospital?' Ahmed cried out. 'To do that we have to go through the checkpoint – the hospital is on the other side. And anyway, I don't have a car. Is there nothing else you can do here?'

'I cannot do any more, but my son Rakesh has a car. It is old but it works. I am sure he will drive you. And the soldiers will let you through the checkpoint when they realize how urgent this is. They, too, are human.'

It was half an hour before the car was at the door. Rosmira was lifted from the bed and placed gently into the back seat of the old saloon. A fine white dust covered the interior of the car. Ahmed climbed in beside his wife and spoke urgently to the driver. 'Go quickly, Rakesh. Quickly, please.'

They set off, the car throwing up clouds of dust as it left the village. Eventually, as they crested a low hill, they saw in the distance the high barbed-wire fence that snaked across the countryside, cutting off their village from the nearby town. Further up the road a queue of cars waited in the heat of the day at the checkpoint, their engines ominously silent. People stood around talking. Up ahead a young soldier was interrogating the driver of the first car.

Ahmed turned and kissed his wife hurriedly on the cheek. 'Wait. I will not be long. I will tell them it is urgent.'

He climbed out of the car and ran along the road towards the checkpoint. The movement drew the attention of the soldier, who stopped his interrogation abruptly. He raised his gun as Ahmed approached.

'Stop,' shouted the soldier. 'Stop, or I'll shoot.'

Ahmed raised his hands as if to calm the soldier's anger and called back. 'Sir, it is an emergency. My wife. She is sick. She needs the hospital. We have to get through now.'

'Wait like the rest,' shouted back the soldier, hardly more than a boy. 'Get back in your vehicle and wait your turn.'

Ahmed hesitated and then turned back, running down the dirt road towards the car.

Inside the car Rosmira was crying out. A small group of women had gathered. Suddenly her cries rose to a scream. One of the women got into the car and knelt on the back seat beside the younger woman. She turned and called to the women standing in the road: 'It is coming. It is coming.'

'Can you see the head?' asked one of the women anxiously.

The woman in the car hesitated for a moment and then called back: 'It is not the head ... it is an arm.' At this there was a great cry of despair from the women at the side of the car.

'What's happening?' shouted Ahmed. 'What's wrong?'

A large woman pushed him firmly back against the hot metal of the car. 'Listen,' she said. 'You must have courage. The baby cannot

75

be born. It is in the wrong position.' Ahmed tried to turn and speak to Rosmira in the car behind him. 'No – do not say anything. Just listen. We must get her to the hospital immediately. Go and talk to the soldiers – and do not get angry. It is important that you do not get angry. Do you hear me? Now go.'

Ahmed hesitated, then raced off up the road towards the checkpoint. As he ran, he was aware of shouting up ahead of him. Men from the cars and people on foot carrying bundles were all shouting at the soldiers.

Ahmed ran up to the crowd. 'Let me through. Please, it is urgent. I must get through.'

'No one is getting through,' said one of the crowd, turning. 'They have just shut the gates. No one is being allowed through the checkpoint until tomorrow.'

It was a dream. The world was spinning. Everything seemed to be happening in slow motion. Nothing seemed real. Ahmed was yelling. A young soldier was shouting at him to be silent. A gun was raised and Ahmed was knocked to the ground.

Far back down the road, two strangers carrying heavy canvas bags were walking slowly towards the queue of traffic. In the back of a car a woman was screaming. An old woman kneeling beside her got out of the car and turned to the others.

'Get a knife,' she said. 'Get it now. We have to cut her.' There was a wail of anguish from the crowd round the old car.

Up ahead two men dragged the half-conscious Ahmed away from the soldier and into the safety of the crowd. 'Let this man through,' shouted someone from the crowd. 'For mercy's sake, his wife is dying.'

The young soldier raised his gun again, in fear as much as in anger. 'You are nothing but vermin. You deserve to die.'

There was a roar from the crowd and the soldier backed away towards the checkpoint. Other young soldiers had emerged into the hot sunlight to see what the noise was about.

Ahmed stumbled back along the road towards the car. Women were shouting and screaming. There was blood. His feet felt like lead.

A woman was standing by the car holding something. Ahmed looked uncomprehendingly at the woman and the lump of raw meat in her hands. There was blood on her dress. Something was dripping into the dust of the road.

The two strangers put down the bags they were carrying and stood watching in horror. The woman held out her bloody offering to the man. He took the tiny body in his hands. It was still warm from the womb. He looked down in incomprehension at his dead child, the heavy, blood-filled placenta still attached by the cord. Then he threw back his head and howled.

He turned to the crowd and saw Goldman and Sheppard. 'You. You Americans did this,' he shouted with all the anger and pain in his body.

There was silence and he turned, walking slowly back up the road holding out the bloody body like an offering. He walked slowly all the way up to the front of the queue of cars. He walked up to the young soldier with the gun.

'Behold my son,' he shouted hoarsely. 'Behold my life.'

Slowly he turned away. A single shot rang out. The man crumpled in a heap on the road, the tiny body spilling, tumbling, falling out of his hands into the road. Grey dust clung to the blood, coating the dead baby's nakedness like meat dipped in flour.

Back down the road the young mother's life was ebbing away. The blood on the car seat was sticky in the heat.

In the distance a car engine started, the sound stirring the crowd as though from a dream. Someone shouted from further up the queue of cars. 'They have opened the gates. We can go through.'

Soon the other cars were gone.

Goldman realized that Sheppard had disappeared. Rakesh was covering the body of the mother on the back seat of his car. His hands trembled as he touched Rosmira's clothing. Tears were streaming down his face.

Up the road Sheppard was walking slowly back towards them. In his arms was the body of Ahmed. Resting across Ahmed's body lay the dead child. Together they put Ahmed's body on the back seat next to the woman for whom this was to have been the most wonderful day. Gently they laid the body of her child in her lap.

Sheppard held the sobbing Rakesh in his arms. 'Take them home,' he said eventually. 'Take them home.'

The two strangers walked in silence, filled with the horror of what they had seen. Finally Goldman spoke. 'What did the guy mean about us being Americans?'

'Our clothes are different,' said Sheppard. 'They guessed we were foreigners. Assumed we were Americans.'

'But why did he say we did this?'

'Think about it,' said Sheppard. 'Western money buys influence. It finances the people with the guns and ensures a secure power base. It protects vested interests – oil in particular. Ring any bells?'

'Meaning what?'

Sheppard shrugged. 'You're the one who told Raffa you had interests in oil. Well, this is where most of it comes from. It's not difficult to work it out.'

'That's the trouble,' said Goldman quietly. 'I have worked it out. This journey's like a wrecking ball smashing everything to pieces.' He paused. 'That's how it's going to be, isn't it? Another hammer blow every day, until I'm destroyed.'

'Plenty of other people are being destroyed. Ask those people back down the road. Why should you be any different?' retorted Sheppard.

'So you're saying that is what's happening to me?' said Goldman.

'That, or something else,' replied Sheppard.

'What do you mean by that?'

Sheppard sighed. 'Give it a break, will you?'

'I need to know,' insisted Goldman.

'All right, I'll tell you. Back at the river when you were bragging to Raphael about all the things you owned, I seem to remember you talking about really big stuff: ships, planes, oil fields – as well as your big house.'

'What's that got to do with anything?' said Goldman.

'Well, have you thought how you'd go about dismantling and carrying an oil tanker – or, come to that, an oil well? And what about the house – what's left of it? Are you really going to take it to pieces and carry it, brick by blackened brick? It's utterly impossible.'

'So what are you saying?'

'That for Raffa to set you a totally impossible task would be inhumane – crazy. And he didn't strike me as being either of those things.'

'No? You don't think this nightmare of a journey is crazy?'

'Not if it has a purpose,' said Sheppard.

'What sort of purpose?'

Sheppard shrugged. 'Who knows?'

A very good man

Over the days and weeks they gradually slipped into a rhythm of walking and sleeping. The bags of coins did not get any lighter and the strain on their arms and shoulders was no easier but, in some strange way, the days passed almost unnoticed. They lost all sense of time.

As they walked, they became aware that it was getting hotter. Much hotter – as though they had entered a different hemisphere. The air had a different smell, perhaps a hint of spices. As though someone far away had opened an oven door. The cloudless sky was a bowl of metallic blue and the sun beat down on the dusty earth. Nothing moved, except for an insect chirping in grass scorched brown by the heat of an African summer.

Ahead, in the distance, a woman was walking slowly at the side of the road, her bare feet stirring puffs of dust with each step. Through the heat haze they could see a vast, sprawling settlement – a sea of huts, shacks and small dwellings made of rough concrete blocks.

As they drew level with the woman she glanced at the two men, a look of placid calm on her face. She wore a brown print dress with a flower pattern on it and, despite the heat of the day, a thick woollen cardigan.

Sheppard raised a hand to his brow in greeting and the woman laughed.

'Very nice,' she said in a soft voice.

'What is nice?' asked Sheppard, as the three walked side by side along the dusty road.

'To meet a respectful man is a very nice thing,' said the woman, smiling. 'And that a white man should greet a black woman in this respectful way is also good. Though I am not sure you are white – perhaps coloured. But your friend is white, I think.' She looked at Goldman. 'Also, it is very unusual for white men to be walking. Mostly they have their cars. But I see you are poor like us. Only the poor walk in this heat.'

'What's this place ahead of us?' said Goldman. 'It looks big.'

'Yes, it is very big. This township is called Constantia. Many, many people live here. Maybe four, five hundred thousand.'

'What happens here?' asked Goldman.

'Nothing happens,' said the woman, this time not smiling. 'Some of us get work far away in the towns and cities, but nothing happens in Constantia.'

'So why is it here?' said Goldman.

'Oh, it is the same story. The white government moved us black people here many years ago. They took us from our homes in the city and dumped us in the desert. They said they were planning a big electric generating plant and they needed a workforce to run it. Large numbers of people would be required, they told us. We believed them, though we had no choice in the matter. But the generating plant was never built and we were left with nothing but the desert.'

'Why didn't you go back to your homes in the city?' asked Goldman.

The woman looked at him for a moment as if undecided whether to answer or not. 'Go back? We were not allowed to go back,' she said quietly. 'Our homes were demolished and the land was taken for the white people who elected the government. There was nowhere to go back to. And so we have been here for many years.'

'That sounds bad,' said Sheppard.

'Yes, it is very bad. There is much violence, especially from the youth. The old people go to church and sing hymns and say we must be patient. But the young people are angry. They are fed up with being poor and living in shacks in the desert. They have guns. They say they want money and jobs and freedom, and they will not wait. Even though we have a black government now, little seems to change.'

'Yet you don't seem unhappy,' said Sheppard.

'No, I am not unhappy. I am one of the lucky ones. I have a job. Every day I get a bus and go into the city. I am a cleaner and childminder for a very nice family.'

'A white family?' asked Sheppard.

'Yes, a white family. But they are kind people. They treat me well and pay me every week. And they call me Auntie Sadie, which is very nice. They have a baby called Sophie who is growing up now. I do child-minding and I love Sophie very much. Very much,' she said, as though savouring the thought.

'So why are you walking and not on the bus today?' asked Goldman.

'That is a very good question,' said the African woman with a big grin. 'I am walking because I am saving up the bus money. It is to buy a toilet for my house. Already I have paid for a man to make the walls and now I have started to pay for some of the pipes. But the pipes are very expensive and so it is taking me a long time to have my toilet. But the walls are built and one day it will all be finished. Then I will be happy. Oh yes, that will be a good day.'

The three walked in silence. The black woman was still smiling, perhaps at the blissful thought of the toilet that would one day be hers.

Goldman realized that he had no idea how many toilets there had been at Tresco. Or how many bedrooms the sprawling mansion had, come to that. The thought made him feel uncomfortable.

'If you like, I will show you my home and where the toilet will be,' said the woman. 'It will be very nice when it is finished.'

As they approached the township, Goldman began to feel apprehensive. Many people greeted them with smiles and waves but some of the younger men, hanging around a drinking place, glared at the white men and the heavy bags they were carrying.

The shebeen owner came out into the harsh sunlight, staring at the three travellers. Hostility crackled like static in the still air.

'We're walking into trouble here,' muttered Goldman.

'Do you know those men, Sadie?' asked Sheppard.

'Yes. Do not worry; they are only boys. But it is better that you are with me. I don't think they will harm you. I know the mothers of two of them, and they are very fierce ladies. These boys know they will be in big trouble if they disrespect me or my friends.' She paused. 'I hope so, anyway.'

Goldman glanced at Sheppard and raised an eyebrow.

They kept walking, not daring to look around. Children in ragged clothing watched the men as they walked past. A thin yellow dog approached and sniffed suspiciously at their legs. Finally, they came to a small one-room house made of concrete blocks. Its corrugated iron roof was red with rust.

Some of the other houses were of the same construction, but most were no more than shacks made of old planks, rusted metal sheeting and plastic bags. A row of communal toilets stood on an area of waste ground, along with a single water tap.

'Welcome to downtown metropolitan Constantia,' muttered Goldman.

Either the woman did not hear his comment or she chose to ignore it. 'It is very hard living here, especially for the poor who live in the shacks,' she said. 'In the winter when the gales come, the sand is blown into their homes. The rain comes in through the roof and it is very cold. Many of them get ill with the cold and the despair. Sometimes there is a fire and people are killed.'

'Are there no hospitals – or fire engines around here?' asked Goldman.

'In the white towns there are. Sometimes they come here if some-one calls on a mobile phone. But even if they do, it is not easy for them to find their way in these streets, which are very narrow, as you can see. So, often, they do not bother to come.'

Suddenly she clapped her hands together as if calling small children to order. 'Now,' she said. 'Let us not be unhappy. Come and see my home and my new toilet walls. And maybe you will stay for a cup of bush tea?'

It was dark inside the house after the glare of the sun, and it took the two men a few moments for their eyes to adjust. The house had a hard earth floor. In the single room was a bed with a blue and white knitted cover and a small wooden table and two old chairs. In one corner was a cupboard, its white paint peeling. On top was a faded red plastic bowl. At the side of this makeshift sink, on another dilapidated cupboard, sat an ancient two-ring electric cooker.

'Please sit down. I will be only a moment,' she said as she went out to fill her tin kettle from the communal tap. A few minutes later she was back and, switching on one of the electric rings, she smiled at her two guests. 'You see, I have a very good home. I have electricity and soon I will have a toilet.'

'A toilet would be good,' agreed Sheppard, nodding thoughtfully. 'It must be difficult without one.'

Sadie raised her hands in a gesture of resignation. 'Ah yes, it is so difficult. I am getting old now and often in the night I need the toilet. But I have to go outside and walk in the dark across to the toilet block. In the winter the weather is bad and the cold is not good for my old bones. Also, it is not safe for a woman to go out in the darkness at night. There are men who do bad things. Bad things. Especially when they are drunk or on tick.'

'Tick?' said Goldman. 'What's that?'

'A drug that makes you forget how hard life is. But it costs much money, so people have to rob and steal to buy it. And that, with the drink, leads many people to do violent things. So you can see, it is not wise for a woman to be out of her home in the dark in her nightclothes. That is why I am having a toilet for my house. Then I can sleep in peace.' And she smiled and nodded calmly to herself at the thought.

When they had drunk the strange bush tea the woman had prepared, they rose to leave, reluctant to be parting from their new friend. Goldman looked round at the rough concrete walls. The worn furniture. In a strange way it reminded him of his childhood, in the good days before the darkness came. It had the same atmosphere of . . . what? Homeliness?

And Sadie? What was it about her? She looked nothing like his mother, who had been fair-haired and slim. Sadie was certainly not that. But there was something. The way she made the tea. Perhaps her optimism. Her warmth. Goldman wanted to reach out and touch her arm, just there in the gentle crease of her elbow where the skin looked so soft.

'Wait for a moment,' said Sadie, breaking into his thoughts. 'I will get someone to go with you to the edge of the township. They will show you the way and make sure that no one harms you. I am glad you have visited my home. It has been very nice to meet you. I hope your journey goes well. Like us here in Constantia, you too have a great burden to carry.'

As they stood at the door, Goldman, on an impulse, stepped forward and hugged the woman. Her body was warm, like his mother's had been. 'I don't want to be rude,' he said, struggling to find the right words, 'but I wondered whether you would let me make a contribution. Towards the toilet – the pipes?'

He pressed something into her hand. The metal glinted in the afternoon light. For a moment it seemed that the woman was going to faint. She bobbed, almost in a curtsey of gratitude, the tears running down her face. 'Thank you,' she said gravely. 'You are a very good man. Very good man.'

A teenage youth appeared at the door, breaking the tension. He glanced warily at the two strangers – then at the heavy bags they were carrying. Goldman sensed mischief, or perhaps danger. The youth caught Goldman's stare and grinned. His front teeth were missing, giving him a strangely evil look. Goldman shuddered.

They picked up their bags and set off, but halfway down the dusty street Goldman stopped and turned. Sadie was still standing at the door of her home. He waved, then turned to join the others.

* * *

Later, when they were on their own, Goldman said, 'Was that OK? The money?'

Sheppard did not look at him but gazed ahead down the road. 'It was a kindness. An unexpected kindness. I didn't think you would do something like that.'

'And?'

'You made her very happy.'

'But there's something else, isn't there? Something you're not telling me.'

'Possibly,' said Sheppard. 'I don't know.'

'Well, at least she'll get her toilet a lot sooner than she would have done,' said Goldman. 'That's something.'

'Perhaps,' said Sheppard.

'Perhaps what?' demanded Goldman.

'Oh, I don't know. I'm just a bit uneasy about what might happen to an elderly woman living alone in a place like that when she suddenly comes into a lot of money.'

Goldman was silent. He thought about Sadie and her toilet and about Sheppard's unease. Giving her the money had brought him unexpected pleasure. Now the sudden realization that he might have put her at risk made him feel sick.

'Anyway, how are your shoulders these days?' asked Sheppard. 'Still aching?'

'They're OK,' said Goldman reluctantly. 'Inasmuch as anything is ever going to be OK.'

'Hey, that's good,' said Sheppard. 'Like I told you, keep your shoulders back and your spine straight. Walk tall.'

Walk tall? Goldman thought to himself. You must be bloody joking.

The rescue

Jean Gregson glanced anxiously at the kitchen clock. She was running late and still hadn't brushed her hair. Hurrying into the bathroom, she caught sight of herself in the mirror.

'Dear heavens, girl, you're getting old,' she sighed. Her once lovely face was now lined with worry and her greying hair desperately needed a trim. She pushed a few strands off her forehead in a vain attempt to repair the ravages of time and years of overwork. She looked around for her lipstick, which seemed to have disappeared in the chaos of the bathroom. She shrugged and walked quickly back to the kitchen.

Closing the blinds to block out the fierce sun, she grabbed her handbag and a bottle of water, together with the car keys. Her sandals clicked on the tiled floor as she walked swiftly to the outer door. Under the shade of the carport she unlocked the battered white Volkswagen and tossed the handbag and water across on to the front passenger seat. She had forgotten to put sunblock on, but there was no time now. One day wouldn't matter anyway.

Stones popped under the tyres as she reversed carefully down the dirt track that led to the road. Suddenly she braked and jumped out of the car. Walking hurriedly back to the house and into the kitchen, she scooped up her phone. Now she really was late.

Out on the open road, she drove fast. There was little traffic, and in a car with air conditioning it would have been a pleasant journey. But a two-hour drive with the temperature in the high thirties would not be fun.

The phone rang. Reaching across to the passenger seat, she picked it up. 'Jean Gregson here.' She spoke in the precise, clipped tones of a South African. 'No, I can't do that. I'm on my way to a meeting.

No.' There was a pause. 'No, she must do it. It is her area ... her responsibility.'

There was another long pause as the person at the other end spoke again. Jean sighed. 'Oh, very well. Yes, I will go ... I will go now. I think I know the place. It is too important to be ... yes ... thank you. Goodbye.' She rang off and put the phone back on the passenger seat.

Glancing ahead she saw a rusty blue minibus, packed with people, careering round a bend towards her. It veered wildly on to the wrong side of the road as the driver fought to keep control. Jean swerved to avoid a collision and the Volkswagen slammed into the verge, throwing up a cloud of dust and stones. There was a loud bang and the steering wheel started to shake wildly. She braked, struggling to keep the car on the road until it came to a grinding halt.

There was silence. The minibus had not stopped. Jean beat her hands on the steering wheel in frustration. Then she got out, unsteadily, and walked round the front of the car. The engine ticked as it began to cool but there was no other sound. She looked at the nearside front wheel. The tyre had been ripped almost off and the steel rim was buckled.

She went to the back of the car and opened the boot. The spare wheel was dirty and heavy. Somewhere there must be a spanner for the wheel nuts. Eventually she found the wheel brace and the jack and carried them round to the front of the car. The sun was hot on her head and shoulders. She had forgotten to bring a hat.

After struggling for a few minutes, she managed to jack the car up, but the wheel nuts refused to budge. She tried putting her foot on the brace to get more leverage, but her thin sandals slipped on the wheel spanner. Eventually she gave up and went to sit in the car.

Picking up the phone, she dialled a number. 'This is Jean Gregson. Yes, I know. I am going to be late. I have a problem with the car. No, I will go and pick up the child. You need to ring the magistrate. We need a temporary order. It has to be done immediately. Yes, I'm fine. Goodbye.'

She put the phone down. She glanced hopefully in the rear-view mirror but there was no sign of any other traffic. She could feel the anxiety building up in her chest. I'm definitely not fine, stuck out here in the middle of nowhere, she thought. She drummed her fingers on the black plastic of the steering wheel, trying to ease the tension. A trickle of perspiration ran down her face. It was getting hotter by the minute.

Back down the road, two figures emerged from the bushes. They stopped as though uncertain which way to go. Then they turned and began walking slowly along the road towards her car. The bags they were carrying looked heavy.

Jean took a drink of water from the bottle, watching the men's progress in the mirror uneasily. A woman stranded out here on her own was not good. She noticed that one of the men walked with a limp and used a stick. He carried one bag over his shoulder and another in his free hand. By the look of his clothes he was one of the many vagrants in the area. The older man was well dressed in a suit and tie that looked slightly ridiculous in the heat of the day. He was also carrying two bags.

As they drew nearer, Jean got out of the car. 'Can you give me a hand?' she said, trying to sound confident. 'I've had a flat and I can't get the wheel off. The nuts seem rusted on.'

Sheppard put his bags down. 'Sure, let's have a look.'

Jean began to relax. Maybe she was not in danger after all.

'I don't suppose you have any water?' Sheppard asked.

'Only this bottle. I've been using it, but you're welcome to have a drink. I don't think you'll catch anything.'

Sheppard grinned. He drank gratefully and passed the bottle to Goldman.

The two went to examine the damaged wheel. Sheppard tried to move the nuts but they were solid. 'Try putting the brace on and then stamp on it,' suggested Goldman. 'Might break the rust seal.'

'My legs are not so good,' said Sheppard. 'Can you have a go?'

Goldman fitted the brace and stamped down hard. At the third attempt there was a sharp squeak of protest. The wheel nut moved fractionally. It was half an hour before the spare wheel was fitted and the damaged one stowed in the boot of the car.

'Thanks,' said Jean. 'I'm not sure how long I'd have been stuck here if you hadn't come by. Can I give you a lift? Where are you heading?'

'We're going the same way as you,' said Sheppard.

'Come far?' asked Jean, as they drove off.

'We were in a place called Constantia a couple of days ago,' said Sheppard.

'Ach, big problems there,' said Jean, lapsing into a thick South African accent.

Sheppard smiled mischievously, his blue eyes twinkling.

'What's funny, man?'

'The way you talk.'

'You want to get out and walk?' said Jean tartly.

'No. I'm sorry – that was rude.'

'Only kidding.' She smiled and patted his knee playfully. She had strong hands, but the brown skin blemishes on them made her seem strangely vulnerable. She glanced across at him. 'You remind me of my son.'

'Do I? What's he like?'

'He's cheeky like you,' she said and laughed.

Sheppard grinned. 'It's strange, but you remind me a bit of my mother.'

'I hope that's not a bad thing,' said Jean, smiling.

'No, not at all. She was great. Fun to be with. She wore the same sort of perfume as you. What is it?'

'Blue Grass,' said Jean. 'My son gives me a little bottle every Christmas.'

There was silence for a few moments, then Sheppard turned to Goldman in the back. 'What was your mum like?' he asked. Goldman said nothing. Instead he hunched down in his seat. Sheppard repeated the question, raising his voice above the noise of the car engine. 'Your mum. What was she like?'

Suddenly Goldman sat bolt upright. 'Just shut up, will you?' he shouted. 'Just shut up and leave me alone.'

'Sorry,' said Sheppard, confused. 'I didn't mean to upset you.'

'There's pain in that boy,' said Jean quietly, glancing across at Sheppard. 'A lot of pain.'

They drove in silence for a long time. Then Goldman said, 'You seem to be in a hurry.' His voice was strained as he tried to sound as if nothing had happened.

'I am in a hurry,' said Jean. She looked in the mirror, hoping he would catch her smile of reassurance, but Goldman was gazing out of the car window at the dry, sun-baked countryside. 'I was already late when I left home and the damaged wheel has made things even worse. I got forced off the road by a taxi. Those minicab drivers are maniacs. No wonder there are so many accidents.'

'Where are you going?' asked Goldman.

'I was supposed to be going to a meeting, but there's been a change of plan. Now I have to go and pick up a baby.'

'Do you collect them?' asked Goldman, leaning forward in the back seat. Jean looked in the mirror. He was smiling now.

'It's beginning to feel like it,' she said grimly. 'I'm with a children's charity. We do child protection. I've just had a call saying there's a baby at risk. I have to go and remove it from danger. The local caseworker can't handle it so, as her manager, I need to step in. Frankly, she's not very good at her job.'

'So why did you hire someone who is no good?' he said.

'Ha. You may well ask. The job was advertised for almost a year on a salary that hardly pays the food bills. Not surprisingly, people weren't queuing up to do an impossible job with a huge workload. In eleven months, we had one application. She was it.'

'So she got the job?'

'It was a choice between appointing someone we knew didn't have the experience needed, or leaving hundreds of vulnerable children with no protection at all.'

'Tough call,' said Sheppard.

'How difficult is it to look after kids?' said Goldman.

'It's not easy here,' said Jean. 'Lots of these kids are sexually abused. Domestic violence is rife. Lots of the children are orphans.

You probably had a happy childhood – but, I tell you, life can be a nightmare for these kids. And there are millions of them. Nobody knows how many – or who they are.'

A happy childhood? Goldman grimaced at the thought of his mother's death – and the father he had so often wished would die. 'Don't you feel like giving up?' he said.

'Never,' replied Jean. 'I may feel like shooting a politician or two, but we'll never give up on the kids.'

They reached the outskirts of a town and Jean pulled over. She wound down the window and greeted a woman, speaking in a language neither Sheppard nor Goldman had heard before. There was a cordial exchange and the woman walked on. As they drove further into the town Jean said, 'I've been here before but I wanted to check my directions, just to make sure.'

'Don't these people speak English?' asked Goldman.

'Most of them speak three or four languages but English isn't their first. I try to use their own language. It's more polite – a sign of respect.' She glanced in the mirror at Goldman. 'How many languages do you speak?' she asked.

'Just English,' said Goldman, embarrassed.

'And the language of money,' said Sheppard.

'Ah, the language of money,' said Jean reflectively. 'An easy language to learn but a difficult one to speak with love, I think.'

There was an uneasy silence, broken by their arrival outside what appeared to be a derelict terraced house. The windows were dirty and some of the panes of glass were broken. Small children played in the litter outside the door and the beat of loud music boomed from the depths of the building. The whole street looked run-down.

'Can you hang on?' said Jean. 'I may be some time – especially if there is trouble.'

'Trouble?' said Goldman. 'What sort of trouble?'

Jean sighed. 'Well, I have to remove a baby from its mother. But the mother, who may be drunk, is likely to be very unhappy about that. There'll probably be other people around who may also see me as an intrusion into their affairs.'

'Will they be violent?' asked Goldman.

'I hope not.'

'What will you do if they are?'

She shrugged. 'Do what I always do. Stay calm and hope for the best.'

She was gone for ten, maybe fifteen minutes. Through the open car windows, Sheppard and Goldman could hear shouting above the sound of the dance music.

'Should we go in?' said Goldman.

'Maybe give it a bit longer,' said Sheppard. 'It might make things worse if we appear on the scene. Anyway, we need to keep an eye on our bags. We don't want them going walkabout.'

'She must have a lot of guts to do this job,' said Goldman.

'You're not kidding.'

Eventually Jean reappeared carrying a small bundle. She was pursued by a young white woman wearing a miniskirt and a low-cut red top screaming abuse at her. Walking briskly to the car, Jean pushed the bundle through the rear window to Goldman. 'Hold on to this – and be careful. It's fragile.'

The woman grabbed a handful of Jean's hair and tried to wrest her away from the car. 'That's my kid, you bitch,' she yelled. 'Give me my fucking baby.'

Jean twisted round and shoved the young woman away from her. The woman tottered backwards on her high heels and fell into the road.

'I'll fucking kill you, you bitch,' she screamed at Jean.

Two men emerged from the building, staggering into the bright sunlight. 'Get her,' the woman yelled, as she scrambled awkwardly to her feet. 'The bitch is running off with my kid. I'll scratch her effin' eyes out when I get her.' Jean jumped into the car and they drove off, leaving the young woman standing in the street shouting.

Jean looked in the mirror. The two men were getting into an old pick-up truck. 'We've got company,' she said.

Sheppard looked back. The pick-up was following them down the dusty street, swerving drunkenly from side to side as it careered after them, its horn blaring. Without warning, there was a shot as one of the men leaned out of the passenger window waving a handgun.

'Keep down,' shouted Sheppard. Goldman ducked low on the back seat, clutching the small bundle in his arms.

Jean took an abrupt left turn. The pick-up tried to follow, but the driver lost control and slammed into a parked car. There was a loud bang. In the rear-view mirror, Jean glimpsed a cloud of steam coming from the truck's radiator. 'That's slowed the idiots down,' she said.

Goldman straightened up uncertainly. 'Are they still following us?'

'No,' said Jean. 'We were lucky. Though they probably wouldn't have caught up with us anyway, the amount of stuff they've been smoking.'

'Are you all right?' asked Sheppard.

'I'm fine – just a bit shaken. I'm sorry about that. It wasn't very professional.'

Goldman looked down at the bundle on his lap. A tiny coffee-coloured face was staring up at him from the filthy blue blanket. He suddenly remembered his own child: the photograph that Trudi had sent him – the baby he had never known. Never held in his arms. 'What am I supposed to do with this thing?' he asked, pulling himself together.

'You seem to be doing fine,' said Jean, looking back at him in the mirror. 'Just hold him the right way up and try not to drop him.'

'OK,' said Goldman, 'but I hope it doesn't leak.'

Sheppard smiled. 'Yes, make sure it doesn't spoil your posh suit. Still, at least that would be preferable to a couple of bullet holes.'

Goldman smiled. 'Where are we going now?' he asked Jean.

'We need to take him to the clinic to get him some medical atten-tion. Then I have to try to find him temporary care until we can sort this mess out.'

'Was it bad in there?' said Goldman, thinking back to the house where they had found the baby.

'Not good. Lots of drink: rough alcohol. And drugs. I tried talking to them but they were completely out of it – apart from one guy with his hands all over Little Miss Sunshine. But at least no one was paying much attention to the baby. He's got some sort of leg injury. He's had a plaster cast on it but someone's removed it – probably using a kitchen knife. There's a small flesh wound where the knife's cut into the leg. We need to get it looked at before infection sets in.'

'But this kid's only a few months old,' said Goldman. 'How does a tiny baby break its leg?'

'He could have been dropped – or perhaps hit with something. Who knows?'

'These people are animals,' said Goldman contemptuously.

'No, they're human beings,' said Jean. 'Trouble is, they've probably been knocked around since they were babies themselves. Then we expect them to behave as if everything's normal. It doesn't work.'

'Why are they so poor?' asked Goldman defensively.

'The system. The people who make the real money are the big corporates and politicians – people with power.'

Goldman said nothing. He looked down at the baby. This is not my fault, he thought to himself.

Moments later the car pulled into a compound surrounded by a steel security fence. The clinic was a converted shipping container. Rust was beginning to show through its white paint. The windows had wire mesh covering the glass.

'Would you like to come in?' Jean said, as they got out of the car.

'We're coming in with him,' said Goldman firmly, cradling the small bundle in his arms. He could feel the warmth of the baby's body through the blanket.

They watched as a nurse unwrapped the tiny child. His limbs were wasted and his head seemed too large for his body. The nurse measured and weighed the baby, inspecting it gently but thoroughly. 'Hmm,' she said. 'Probably eight or nine months, though he's only half the weight he should be. Very hungry. Definitely needs a bath and a good mother.'

'Why is his head like that?' asked Sheppard.

'Alcohol,' said the nurse. 'The mother must have been drinking heavily while she was pregnant. The foetus was damaged by the alcohol. That means more problems in the future.'

'Is it common?' asked Goldman, looking anxiously at the small child who was gazing wide-eyed at the circle of faces above him.

'Unfortunately, yes,' said the nurse.

Jean interrupted. 'We need to take a break and get some food. Will you look after him for now?'

'Of course,' said the nurse. 'He looks basically OK, but we need to feed him. And that may take some time. I don't suppose you have a name for him?'

'Afraid not,' said Jean. 'The mother forgot to mention it.'

The nurse chuckled. 'What's your name?' she asked Goldman. 'Your first name.'

'Harry.'

'OK, we'll call him Harry. After all, it was you who brought him here. You don't mind, do you?'

Goldman shook his head but said nothing. He pulled out a grubby handkerchief and blew his nose. Jean caught Sheppard's eye. 'Come on,' she said. 'Time to eat. And it's my treat. You guys have earned it.'

* * *

Hours later, when the two men were back on the road and the town was far behind them, Goldman said, 'Are they really going to call him Harry?'

'Probably,' said Sheppard. 'Would it matter?'

'I was never very interested in kids,' Goldman said, avoiding the question.

'Did you never have children?' asked Sheppard.

Goldman hesitated. 'Yes, but he lived with his mother. He died.'

'And this brought back a few memories?'

'I suppose so.'

'Are you glad they're calling him Harry?'

'Yes – a bit.'

'I thought you might be,' said Sheppard.

'You think I'm getting soft, don't you?'

'What's wrong with soft?'

'It leaves you vulnerable, that's what. You let your guard down and people attack you. Like the things Jean was saying about money and power. Don't think I didn't notice. It's like every day I get hit with something else I got wrong. I tell you, this stuff is destroying me.'

'Really?' said Sheppard. 'Watching you with that baby, it didn't seem that way at all. I had the feeling something else was happening.'

'Well, I'm going to be tough from now on,' said Goldman.

'Tough?' said Sheppard, grinning. 'You don't know the meaning of the word. Listen, I once knew a woman who ate nails – now that's what I call tough.' He paused. 'Of course, she boiled them first.'

'You're a nutcase,' said Goldman.

'Well, at least it got a smile out of you.'

They walked in an easy silence for a long time. Occasionally Goldman would stop and look back the way they had come.

'What's up?' said Sheppard.

'Nothing. I had the feeling something was following us.'

'Like there was in the woods?'

'Maybe. I'm not sure.'

'I thought you were managing to put that nightmare stuff behind you.'

'Well, I've been better these last few weeks, haven't I?'

'Yes,' said Sheppard. 'Now I think about it, I suppose you have.'

An unexpected outcome

It was a long time before Sheppard noticed the change in Goldman's breathing. Earlier they had come to the brow of a hill. Goldman, relieved that their long climb had come to an end, bounded headlong down the slope. Still clutching his heavy bags, he whooped with delight, like a five-year-old allowed out to play. As he came to the bottom of the slope, he had stumbled on the uneven tufts of grass and yelped in pain. But the moment passed and the pair carried on walking.

An hour or so later, Sheppard became aware that the other man was in distress. Each step brought a gasp of discomfort. Sheppard turned and looked back to Goldman, struggling a few paces behind him. 'What's wrong?'

'My hip. I pulled something when I ran down that hill.'

'Does it hurt?'

'Only when I walk.'

Sheppard frowned. 'I'm not sure what to do about that. We could rest for a while.'

They halted for almost an hour before Goldman said, 'It's no good; we have to push on. Let's just take it slowly.'

It was nearly nightfall before they came to the settlement. In what appeared to be the village square, a young woman was locking the door of a small wooden church. She turned and saw the two men. 'Good evening. Are you OK? You look tired.'

Her hair was bleached by the sun and had been neatly plaited into rows of thin braids. She wore a thin green cotton shift and a bracelet made of tiny coloured beads shone bright against her tanned skin.

'My friend's pulled a muscle in his hip,' said Sheppard. 'Is there a medical centre where we can get it looked at?'

'There isn't a doctor, but we have a hospice with a nurse who might be able to help.' She glanced at her watch. 'She's probably still there – let's go and see.'

The woman led them down a quiet side street until they came to a long wooden shed that constituted the hospice. In a small office a black woman in a nurse's uniform was typing at a computer. She turned as the three stepped into the room.

'Leylani, can you help these men? One of them has an injured hip.'

'Are you on a long journey?' asked the nurse.

'For ever,' muttered Goldman.

'Pardon?'

'A long trek,' said Sheppard. 'And still quite a way to go.'

'Your bags look heavy. Can you not get a lift?'

'Our route goes across country quite a bit. Is there anything you can do to ease the problem?'

'All I have is painkillers,' said the nurse, going to a cupboard. 'I can give you a few, but we can't spare a lot. They'll help you for a day or two. You need to keep it exercised, but don't put too much pressure on it.'

Goldman wondered how he was going to carry two heavy bags over open ground without putting pressure on it. 'Thanks,' he said, unconvinced.

As they left the hospice, the young woman from the church said, 'You must be hungry after your travelling. Do you want something to eat – and perhaps stay the night? It gets dark quickly here and there are no street lights.'

'That's kind of you,' said Sheppard. 'Are you always so welcoming to strangers?'

'We don't get many people passing this way,' said the woman. 'But in any case, you seem like good people.'

As they shared a simple meal, Sheppard said, 'I'm sorry, but we never asked your name.'

'Rachel,' said the young woman. 'I'm the minister at the church here.'

'You don't look like a vicar,' said Goldman.

Rachel laughed. 'No, I don't suppose I do. I'm just not very good at conforming. I wasn't brought up in the Church. All that dark and gloomy stuff doesn't appeal to me. And I'm not sure God's very keen on it either.'

'You seem to get on well with the people at the hospice,' said Sheppard.

'The church runs the hospice,' said Rachel. 'Would you like to meet some of our patients?'

'People who are dying?' said Goldman.

'Yes, we'd like that,' cut in Sheppard. 'It'll take our minds off other things.'

Rachel smiled. 'These people don't often see new faces. It'll be a nice change for them.' She paused. 'You don't have a problem with the idea of people dying, do you?'

The two men glanced at each other. 'No,' said Sheppard. 'We're OK with that.'

Despite their outward confidence, the appearance of the very sick patients in the ward came as a shock. As they walked down the long wooden hut, they exchanged quiet greetings with the people in the beds. Goldman found it strangely moving, though he wasn't sure why.

As they came to the end of the ward, Rachel paused for a moment. 'There is one other patient. She's in a separate room. Her name is Fezeka and she is close to death. She's very special. She has a young daughter and I've been arranging foster care for her when her mother dies.'

'How long has Fezeka got?' asked Goldman.

'She's unlikely to make it through the night,' said Rachel. 'Her husband's with her now. The little girl's already gone to stay with the foster-mother. She'll be looking after her from now on. It's very sad but it happens a lot. We just hope the father keeps in touch with the child.'

Sheppard frowned slightly. 'If her husband's with her, it seems wrong to barge in, especially if she is so ill.'

Rachel thought for a moment. 'Yes, I know. But death can be such an isolating experience. I'll ask them if they'd like to see you. Give me a minute.'

The two men stood in the doorway of the small room as Rachel went in. A woman lay motionless in the bed, her head propped up on a pillow. She was so thin that the white sheets were hardly raised by the outline of her body. Disease had drawn the skin tight against the bones of her face. A man sat at the side of the bed, his head in his hands.

The husband looked up with a dazed expression as Rachel entered. Goldman and Sheppard could see that he was crying. Rachel raised her hand to the man in greeting and walked over to the bed. She bent over the woman with a warm intimacy, their faces almost touching. The woman smiled and raised her hand, caressing Rachel's braided hair gently. Rachel whispered something and kissed the woman softly on the temple. Straightening up, she spoke to the husband and he answered in the local dialect.

Rachel turned to Sheppard and Goldman in the doorway. 'He says please come in. He does not want her to die alone. He has no family to grieve with him.'

As she stepped back from the bed, Goldman gasped. There was a long scar down the side of the dying woman's face, but despite the injury she was incredibly beautiful.

'It almost makes it worse, doesn't it?' said Rachel. 'In truth it does not matter what she looks like, but somehow her beauty makes her death seem more tragic than it would otherwise be.'

'What happened to her face?' asked Goldman. 'It looks as though she's been slashed with a knife. Was it him?'

'Her husband? No – though he blames himself for what happened. He went away to find work, as do most of the men round here. At first he sent money home, but then it seems he got involved in some trouble. As a result he ended up in prison. Fezeka had a child to feed and no income. Then, one day, a man came and offered her money – in exchange for sex. What else could she do? She ended up working the big hotels in the city. It was good money – for the pimp. One day she ran away, but the man came after her. There was a fight. It seems he raped her. Then he slashed her face. He said he'd make sure no one ever wanted her again. Eventually, somehow, she found her way back here. The following year, when the husband was released from prison, she was already very ill with AIDS. Without money they couldn't afford the drugs she needed. By the time she was brought here it was too late. The husband says if he had not gone away she would not be dying. The trouble is, he's probably right.'

Goldman seemed lost in a dream. He thought of all the women who had been provided for him on his many business trips – and the woman in the pub. What was it he had called them? Slappers, tarts, women who want to make a bob or two on their backs. He realized that his fists were clenched with the tension. 'Can nothing be done?' he whispered.

'Oh yes,' said Rachel. 'We can pray. The husband is praying and I am praying and the people in the village are praying. And Leylani continues giving her the antiretroviral drugs, even though it is far too late for them to make any difference.'

'Even though there is no hope?' asked Goldman.

'Yes, even when there is no hope,' said Rachel. 'Even when there is no hope, we pray. That is what we do.'

Goldman stepped forward and hesitatingly touched the hand of the dying woman. He felt the bones through the thin skin with a sense of shock. The woman opened her dark brown eyes. He saw they were full of sadness. The eyes of a person who has already left this world. Her hand was trembling.

The woman said something, her voice the faintest whisper.

'What did she say?' he asked.

'She said her daughter's name. She knows she will not see her again.'

Goldman glanced back at the woman in the bed. A tear ran down her beautiful black face and soaked into the whiteness of the pillow. He turned to Rachel. 'We should go.'

She nodded. As they turned away, the husband rose and walked round the bed to them. There was a moment of silence. Then he opened his arms and embraced Goldman. He said something, but Goldman could not understand. Goldman looked hopelessly across at Rachel.

'He says he thanks you for being with him as his life ends,' she said, and the tears were running down her face also. 'He says he can see from your clothes that you are a very important man. You have given him strength and he is grateful.'

Important? thought Goldman bitterly. It was as though a knife had suddenly been driven deep into his guts. No, not any more. In fact, not ever.

As they quietly left the room, Goldman glanced back once more at the dying woman. Her dark eyes were open and she was looking at him, an expression of peaceful calm on her face. Even in death, she was exquisitely beautiful. He turned and joined the others in the open ward.

'Why is this happening? To people like her?' he asked as they walked.

'Why?' said Rachel. 'Poverty, of course. It destroys families and leaves people vulnerable. Then, when they get hit by something like AIDS, the drug companies block cheap medication so they can make bigger profits. Do you know much about international trade?'

Goldman was silent.

She stopped and turned to the two visitors. 'I'm sorry, I shouldn't have gone on like that. But I get so angry about it.'

'You said she was very special to you,' said Sheppard.

Rachel hesitated. 'Fezeka and I have a lot in common,' she said. 'I did not have a happy home life as a child. My stepfather was not a kind man. Nor were friends of his who took an unhealthy interest in me. She and I both carry the scars of our past – as you carry yours.'

As they left the hospice, Rachel continued: 'You were surprised that I don't dress as other clergy. There are good reasons for that. Apart from expressing who I am, it helps me bond with the other women here. We do each other's hair and share our stories. We make bracelets like this one I am wearing. Our time together is a way of saying that women matter. That we are people of value, people of joy – and we will not be crushed, no matter what men may do to us.'

The three walked on in thoughtful silence. It was almost dark.

'Anyway, let me show you where you can sleep,' she said. 'It probably won't be what you're used to, but at least it'll be dry and the night is warm. Tomorrow you must eat before you go – and I promise not to lecture you any more!'

* * *

The morning was sunny but cool. As they emerged from the hut where they had slept, they saw Rachel across the dusty street. She waved and walked over. Her first words were unexpectedly direct. 'Come quickly,' she said.

As they walked back towards the hospice building, Goldman said, 'Has Fezeka died?'

Rachel looked worried, but said nothing. They walked into the open ward and past the rows of beds.

'What is it? What has happened?' asked Sheppard, trying to keep pace with Rachel who was hurrying down the room.

'You'll see,' she said over her shoulder.

They came to the private room, and Rachel pushed open the door. The bed was empty. For a moment the two men were filled with sorrow. Then they realized that someone was sitting in a chair by the window. The beautiful young woman turned. She looked at Goldman and Sheppard and, with great dignity, nodded. She was smiling.

The husband laughed at the shock on their faces and shouted something.

'What does he say?' asked Sheppard.

'He says you have brought them life. They call it *ubuntu*: it means we find life in the other.'

'What happened?' asked Goldman, when they were back in the main ward.

'We don't know exactly,' said Rachel. 'It's a mystery. During the night her blood count unexpectedly began to rise. We don't understand how it's happened, but her body's started to respond to the drugs. She's started to live again. She will see her daughter after all.'

As the two men gathered their bags and prepared to leave, Rachel said, 'We're so glad you came. The husband says that you brought a miracle into their lives. Whatever it was, we're glad you visited us. I hope your journey goes well and you reach your destination – both of you.'

As they turned to go, Sheppard paused. 'Rachel, what's wrong? This is wonderful news, and yet you seem worried.'

'Not worried,' she said. 'But I do have a problem. Last night that woman was dying. Today she is alive and there is great joy. So now I have to go and tell the foster-mother that she will not be able to keep the beautiful child she thought would become her daughter. I have to tell her that the little girl's mother who was dying is not dead. I have to ask her to let go of this new joy in her life. And that will not be easy.'

She glanced at Goldman. His face was wet with tears. She walked over and put her hand on his arm to comfort him. 'You are a good man,' she said.

Goldman pulled away, filled with despair. He wanted to cry out. Scream.

Instead he simply shook his head. 'No. You're wrong,' he said bitterly. 'So wrong.'

'I don't think I am,' she replied.

The crocodile man

Another day of walking, another day of heat. Goldman was having increasing difficulty with the physical demands of the journey. He wondered whether it would ever end. The painkillers had run out days ago and every step was agony as he staggered on under the weight of the bags.

Eventually, Sheppard gave him his stick and the shoulder bag. They had long since run out of water, and Goldman's mouth was dry from the dust. They passed a woman begging at the roadside. A child was with her.

Far off, down the road, they could see a group of people sitting in the shade of a large tree, sheltering from the hot sun. As they approached, thin and almost naked children came uncertainly towards them. Their eyes seemed large and their bellies swollen.

'They want food,' Sheppard said.

Goldman did not reply. The damaged muscle in his hip was giving him so much pain, he could think of nothing else.

As they drew level, a tall man stepped out of the shade of the tree. He wore an old checked shirt and ragged trousers. His feet were bare.

'Water? Have you any water?' asked Sheppard. He gestured with his hand raising an invisible cup to his mouth. 'Water?' he repeated.

'Yes, I understand you,' said the man, speaking with a heavy accent. 'We have water. Not a lot, but some.'

'May we have a small drink?' asked Sheppard. 'My friend and I have been travelling all day. We're very thirsty.'

The tall man did not smile. A small child came up and stood beside him shyly, a scrap of blue rag in its hand. The man continued to look at the two strangers thoughtfully. He turned to the others under the tree and called out to them in the local dialect. The words were interspersed with clicking sounds.

A woman in the crowd shouted in reply, her voice hard and strong. She spoke with authority. There was hostility in her voice. Goldman felt uneasy at what might happen.

'She says we will not help you,' said the tall man. 'She is the Mother and she speaks for all of us.' He paused. 'I am sorry.' He seemed reluctant to convey this information but there was no hesitation in his acceptance of the woman's decision.

'That's strange,' said Sheppard, as if probing to uncover a mystery. 'Other people have met us with courtesy, but your people seem hostile. It is the custom to treat strangers with hospitality, yet you refuse us even a sip of water. Surely we have done you no harm?'

The man turned and spoke to the woman. She stood up and walked towards them. She was dressed in a bright red and yellow kaftan and was surprisingly young.

The woman spoke briefly to the man, who translated for Sheppard and Goldman. 'She says they will not help the crocodile man. He has killed too many people.'

Sheppard glanced at Goldman, who was feeling increasingly uncomfortable.

'Crocodile man?' said Sheppard. 'I don't know what you mean.'

The woman spoke again, the clicking in her words adding force to what she was saying to the tall man.

'She says he is the crocodile man and for that reason we will not help him. Even if he was dying we would not help him.'

'We don't know what you are talking about,' said Sheppard in exasperation. 'We have nothing to do with crocodiles – we are simply travellers with a long way to go and we need –'

His words were interrupted by Goldman falling heavily to the ground. Sheppard threw down his bags and knelt beside him. 'Are you OK?'

Goldman's face was drawn with the pain. 'No. Not really.'

Sheppard stood up and confronted the tall man and the woman. 'Now listen. This man is hurt and he's dehydrated. He's not a crocodile, and we know nothing about crocodiles. We need a drink of water – one drink of water, that's all we're asking for. Then we'll be on our way.'

The woman spoke without waiting for his words to be translated.

'She says you may have a drink of water,' said the tall man.

A young girl came forward with a cup. Goldman sat up. He took a mouthful of the water, then spat it out in disgust. 'It's filthy,' he muttered. 'Tastes dreadful.'

'That is what we have to drink,' said the man. 'You asked for water; that is our water. You say it is filthy, and it is. That is what our children have to drink. That is why they get ill and die. So drink or do not drink, it is your choice.'

Sheppard stepped forward and put his hand on the man's shoulder. He bowed his head in apology. 'I am sorry,' he said. 'We did not intend to be ungrateful. Please forgive us.' He turned to Goldman. 'Try to drink a little. You need the fluids in your body. They drink it and survive, so it can't be too bad.'

Goldman looked doubtful. He took an apprehensive sip of the water.

Sheppard turned to the tall man. 'What do you mean by all this crocodile stuff you're talking about?'

The woman spoke, again not waiting for Sheppard's words to be translated. Again her tone was forceful. As she spoke, she pointed accusingly at Goldman. When she had finished, the man said, 'She says he is a rich man. She can tell by his expensive clothes, even though they are stained and worn. She knows he is the crocodile man.'

'I don't understand,' said Sheppard.

'The crocodile comes and eats our children, it eats our young men, it eats our mothers and our fathers. No matter how much it eats, it is never satisfied. Always it wants more.' He paused and looked at the uncomprehending expressions on the faces of Goldman and Sheppard.

'You do not understand? Very well, I will explain to you. The Mother says that the crocodile has two jaws. If you are caught between the two jaws, you will die. The lower jaw of the crocodile is money. Rich men like your friend here run big businesses. These businesses come to our country and steal our minerals, our crops and our wealth. Then they rob us by not paying the taxes that are due to our government.'

The man pointed at Goldman. 'And so it is the poor who pay the price.'

Goldman shook his head wearily.

'You may shake your head,' said the tall man. 'You may think I am telling you a sermon like a preacher in a pulpit, and maybe I am. But it is time you started to hear the voices of those you have made poor.'

'You said there were two jaws of the crocodile,' said Sheppard, cutting in. 'What's the other one?'

'Do we want more bad news?' said Goldman despondently. 'Let's just clear off out of here.'

Sheppard shrugged. 'We might as well hear the worst.'

'The greed of the rich is one jaw of the crocodile,' said the tall man. 'The other is the weather. It has changed. We are sheltering from the sun under this tree, but it was not always so hot. Sometimes we had bad years when the crops were scorched by the sun, but it was not like it is now. The climate has changed.'

'And have I made the weather change?' demanded Goldman angrily. 'Is that my fault as well?'

'Yes, it is your fault. You and people like you. The weather is changing because of the pollution you create. From your factories and your cars. And so the upper jaw of the crocodile comes down from the sky and crushes us to death. Between the money and the weather we are dying. That is why the Mother said we would not give you water to drink. So that, for a moment, you will know what it is like to be in need and to have people say "no" to you when you beg for their help. For a moment, you will know how we feel every day of our lives.'

'I'm sorry,' said Sheppard. 'We will go on our way.'

Goldman was sitting in the road with his head in his hands. He said nothing.

The tall man spoke again. 'The Mother says you may go when you have eaten with us and she has taken a look at your friend's back. We are people of hospitality, despite our hard words to you.'

Goldman looked up. 'It doesn't matter about the words. But tell the lady my back is not the problem. It is my leg that hurts.'

The woman walked over to him. She was not smiling. 'The pain is in your leg but the problem is in your back,' she said in perfect English. 'It is like the world. The pain is in one place, but the cause is somewhere else. Now, turn over and let me look.'

Goldman turned over and lay face down in the road. The woman knelt beside him. She pulled up his jacket and shirt. Her hands were black against his pink skin. She felt with her fingers for a few moments, as if searching for something in his flesh. Then she leaned her weight forward, her thumbs pressing hard into his back. There was a click, and Goldman gave a howl of pain.

'Sit up now,' she said.

'I can't,' said Goldman.

'Yes, you can,' she replied. 'Don't be a baby. Do as I say.'

Goldman rolled over and sat up tentatively. His face was streaked with tears from the pain.

The woman remained kneeling beside him. 'What's the matter?' asked Goldman.

'I was just thinking,' said the woman. 'Here we are in the dust of the road. And do you know what happens now?' She did not wait for his reply. 'We stand up together. That is how it should be in the world. Your race and my race: your people and my people. We stand together.'

Goldman struggled to his feet, fearful that the pain would return. The woman held out a hand to help him. 'Come now,' she said. 'Dry your eyes. You are not a child.'

She paused as if someone had spoken to her. 'No,' she said thoughtfully, 'I am wrong. You are a child. A child that has been hurt, a long time ago. Perhaps that is why you have become what you are. There is another pain in you: one that I cannot reach. But at least your leg will be well.' She turned away. 'Come. Come and have some food. And we will try to find you some water that is not so dirty.'

As Goldman followed her, the child with the scrap of blue cloth was standing close by, watching. Goldman realized that for the first time in days the pain was gone. He glanced uncertainly at the child. The child smiled.

'Why didn't you say you could speak English when we arrived?' asked Goldman as they ate. 'Were you trying to humiliate us?'

She shrugged. 'Perhaps it was to allow you to discover something. Something about power. About having to speak through an intermediary to survive.'

'So do we understand now?' asked Sheppard.

'How is the food?' she asked. 'And the water?'

'They're good.'

'Then you have begun to understand,' she said.

Goldman realized that the woman was younger than he had thought. 'What's your name?' he asked.

The woman laughed. 'My name is Farina.'

'Is that an African name? It sounds more like French or Italian.'

'You are right. That's very good,' she said. 'My mother chose the name. One day she saw it printed on the side of a wooden packing case and she liked the sound of it. People told her it meant "flower", and she was pleased to think that her daughter would have such a beautiful name. It was very funny.'

'Why funny?' asked Sheppard, confused.

'Because, as your friend says, Farina is an Italian word. It means "flour". Flour for making bread.'

They all laughed.

'But to be called Flour is not so bad. After all, it is the staple of life,' she said. 'And so I am happy to be called by that good name.'

The window cleaner

'OK,' said Goldman. 'Tell me.'

'Tell you what?' asked Sheppard, who was sitting beside him. Despite the warm evening they had lit a fire in the hope of keeping the mosquitoes and other biting insects at bay.

'Tell me what the hell is going on,' said Goldman. 'This journey seems to be leading nowhere. We're following a route we certainly never took on the way to Tresco. We've been walking for weeks, if not months, not knowing where the hell we are. And every day brings another kick in the balls. Every day another reminder of what a shit I am. I want to know what's going on. Is that too much to ask?'

'And you think I have all the answers?' said Sheppard.

'I wouldn't put anything past you,' said Goldman. 'Listen, if you know what this is all about, tell me.'

'Do you believe in coincidences?' asked Sheppard.

'What have coincidences got to do with anything? But since you ask, I don't. I don't believe in anything.'

'Oh, really?' said Sheppard, grinning. 'I thought you believed in money.'

'That's different,' said Goldman. 'Anyway, seriously, what do you mean about coincidences?'

'Ever heard of a guy called Escobar?' asked Sheppard.

'Don't tell me any more stories,' sighed Goldman. 'The last one ended up with someone being eaten alive by dogs. And I'm pretty sure you meant it to be me.'

'Not at all,' said Sheppard amicably. 'As I recall we were discussing the merits of hunting. All I was doing was offering you a slightly different perspective on the subject.'

'With me as the bad guy,' said Goldman.

Sheppard shrugged. 'Look, do you want to hear what happened to our friend Escobar or don't you?'

'What choice do I have?'

'Well, we could always sit here and compare mosquito bites.'

'I'll go for the guy with the funny name,' said Goldman reluctantly.

'Right,' said Sheppard. 'Listen up, as they say. This Escobar was a great military leader. A general. He was famous throughout the land – and feared by the people because he was so powerful. Even the king was in awe of him. There was only one problem. General Escobar had a horrible skin disease. For a long time he tried to hide it, but the papers finally got hold of the story that he was a leper. And everybody knew that it was easier to raise the dead than to heal a leper. The king was horrified because he knew that, apart from anything else, if the general was forced to resign, the army would lose a great leader. The best doctors were called in, but no one could cure him. In fact, the skin disease got steadily worse.'

'Tell me this is leading somewhere,' said Goldman grimly.

'Shut up and listen,' said Sheppard. 'It happened that one day the king's sister heard about a wise woman who had the power to cure this terrible disease. "I will go and see this woman," said General Escobar. And taking a squad of his special bodyguard, he set off to the village where the wise woman lived. Naturally, as his staff car and the jeeps carrying his special troops pulled up outside the woman's house, a crowd gathered to see what was going on. A window cleaner, who happened to be washing the upstairs windows, scrambled down his ladder and ran indoors to tell the woman what was happening. "Have you finished the windows already?" she said. "How much do I owe you?" "Never mind that," said the window cleaner. "Half an army is parked outside your house and there's a guy with a very ugly face who wants to see you. He says you have to come outside and talk to him. Now." The woman walked over to the window and peered from behind the curtains. "Ah yes, I've been expecting him," she said quietly. "You must go and give him a message. Tell him he has to do something very important." "What is that?" asked the window cleaner. "He has to go and jump in the river," she said, smiling.

'The window cleaner was by this time very frightened. "In your dreams, grandma," he shouted. "I'm paid to clean your windows, not get myself shot. You can go and tell him that yourself." The wise woman looked at the window cleaner very sternly. "Just do as I say. Go and tell him to jump in the river." The window cleaner was not sure whether he was more afraid of the general with his soldiers and their guns or of the wise woman, who could be extremely fierce. He shrugged. "OK. I'll go. But if they shoot me, you can clean your own windows." As he walked to the door the wise woman called after him. "Seven times." "Seven times what?" said the window cleaner. "He has to jump in the river seven times." "Get lost," said the window cleaner under his breath as he walked out of the door to what he knew would be certain death.

'"Well?" demanded the general. "Where is the woman?" "She says she will not come out to speak to you," the window cleaner said. "Is that all? Was there no message?" The window cleaner hesitated. "She said you have to jump in the river," he said very quietly.

'At this the soldiers all pointed their guns at the window cleaner and looked as though they might kill him. At least, that is what the window cleaner thought. "Jump in the river?" shouted Escobar. "Is that what the old fool said? Does she know who I am?" The window cleaner said nothing. "Well?" shouted the general. "Did she say anything else?" "She said that you have to do it seven times," whispered the window cleaner.

'For a moment the soldiers thought that the general would order them to kill him. But instead he burst out laughing. "This is nonsense," he shouted. "These people are all fools. We return home." Then, just as the general's car and the army jeeps were reversing in the road, throwing up clouds of dust, General Escobar's personal servant ran up to him and saluted. "Sir," he said. "Please think about this for a moment. If the wise woman had told you to do some heroic deed to be cured of your illness, would you have done it?" The general thought for a moment. "Perhaps," he said. "So why not do what she says – even though it is an easy thing to do?" asked the servant. "Easy?" snapped the general. "This is not an easy thing. It is the hardest thing in the world. To make myself look foolish in front of my men, not to mention this window cleaner and the rest of these peasants? I would rather die." The servant shrugged. "But if you wish to be healed? And if it demands greater courage?"'

'So what happened?' said Goldman.

'The general went to the river,' said Sheppard. 'And the soldiers of his special bodyguard went with him. And the window cleaner and most of the village followed them.'

'And?' said Goldman.

'He went down into the water. Seven times. And it was not a very clean river. And he was healed.'

'Well, hooray,' said Goldman sarcastically. 'Now tell me what the hell that's got to do with us.'

'He had to go down into the river seven times,' said Sheppard.

'So?'

Sheppard sighed. 'Look, just for once, put yourself in another person's position. The general drives down to the river followed by his squad of special guards. They get out of their vehicles and clear the area. "No one must see this," says the general, who is deeply ashamed of his skin disease. So they form a cordon round him on the river bank. Then it occurs to him that he has to take off his uniform. As he gets undressed he takes off his army boots. But the servant says, "I think you need to keep your boots on, sir. There may be broken glass and other rubbish in that water."

'So the general strips off and starts wading out into the river. And, indeed, there is all sorts of rubbish in the water. But the general is a man of courage and he keeps on walking. No one dares look as he goes down under the water the first time, even though he is a very strange sight, because he is wearing only his army boots and his underpants. But the second time, one or two of the soldiers do sneak a look. And they see that some of the villagers have gone over the bridge to the other side of the river to watch. When the general comes up out of the water a third time, the villagers start to shout insults and tell him he should stay under for a very long time. And the fourth time he goes under, they are yelling with glee at this great man who is washing himself in their not very clean river.

'But the fifth time he goes under, someone starts saying that maybe he will catch typhoid from the dirty water and die. And the sixth time he goes under, some people start cheering because they think the general is perhaps not such a bad guy and, whatever else, he has a lot of guts. And the soldiers begin to think that maybe they will not be ordered to shoot the villagers after all. And the seventh time he goes under the water, it seems like this ordeal is lasting for all eternity. And the crowds are beginning to feel truly sorry for this foreign army commander who is doing this crazy thing, exactly as the wise woman tells him. Unless, of course, the window cleaner made it all up.

'And so, when the general comes up out of the water for the last time, everybody starts cheering and yelling with delight – including the soldiers of his special bodyguard who have decided they love this guy more than they can say.'

'And?' said Goldman.

'Escobar comes out of the water and puts his uniform on.'

'And?'

'He is cured of the great fear he has always had: that to be respected he needs to frighten and kill people. And as he looks at the crowd and at his men, he knows he has their respect. And, like I said, his skin is no longer diseased.'

'Well?' said Goldman. 'That is all very well, but what has it got to do with us? And what's this coincidence you were on about?'

'I was thinking about how many times Escobar had to go down into the water,' said Sheppard, 'and how many things have happened to you.'

'What do you mean?' said Goldman.

'Well. There was the man whose wife died at the checkpoint, and Sadie's toilet. And there was the little kid Jean rescued, and the beautiful young woman who was dying. And then there were the people who thought you were a crocodile.' He paused. 'You're good with numbers. How many things is that?'

'Five,' said Goldman.

'Five,' said Sheppard. 'Hmm . . . that's what I was afraid of.'

'You said the story had a happy ending,' said Goldman.

'It did – for Escobar.'

'And what about me?' demanded Goldman.

'What about you?' said Sheppard.

Goldman was silent for a long time. An idea was beginning to dawn on him. 'This guy who had to dip in the river. You said he was cured of the fear that the only way to be respected was to frighten and kill people.'

'So?'

'So why can't what happened to him happen to me? Maybe it's already happened. Maybe this stuff is all over?'

Sheppard sighed. 'I don't think it is, my friend.'

Disaster

Goldman was dreaming. A cold finger touched his forehead. He opened his eyes. Another drop of dew fell on to his face from the branch above. He shivered. The panic began to ebb away. Sheppard was sleeping silently, oblivious to what was happening in the darkness.

Goldman lay awake, thinking. Then he got silently to his feet and felt around for one of the bags. He took out his handkerchief and spread it on the ground. Taking a handful of coins, he wrapped them in the grubby rag and stuffed them in his jacket pocket.

Sheppard stirred, disturbed by the coins clinking. For a moment Goldman thought he would wake, but he grunted in his sleep and was quiet again.

Silently, one step at a time, Goldman crept out of the clearing. There was a gap in the cloud; by the faint moonlight he was able to make out the track, pale against the darkness of the undergrowth. Branches and brambles snatched at his clothes and scratched his face.

He thought about the fear of the early days that something had been following him, watching him. He realized that he had not felt that fear for a long time. In fact he had completely forgotten about it. He smiled to himself, almost giddy with relief.

He walked steadily until daylight, and then some more. He was not sure whether he was heading in the right direction or not. Not certain where he was going at all. But somehow it didn't matter. Somewhere, far off, he thought he could hear someone singing.

Eventually the track joined a dirt road that dropped down the hillside. Ahead was a road junction. On the other side of the junction the ground fell away. Among some trees a ramshackle squatter camp had been set up by a dried-out river bed.

Without warning, a man stepped out in front of him, barring his way. He was wearing an old brown leather jerkin with a torn sleeve and canvas trousers worn through at the knees. But it was his face that rooted Goldman in horror. The man's left eye was missing and the blind socket, red with infection, glared out at him angrily.

The man pressed a knife hard against Goldman's chest. 'What do you want here, stranger?'

Goldman stepped back in terror. 'Nothing, I want nothing.'

'Then why are you here?'

'I was looking for someone. A family. A woman and a child. We saw them begging. A week ago – or maybe more. I'm not sure now. I can't remember.' Goldman was confused. Was it a week ago or a month? Everything seemed out of focus.

'Begging?' said the man. He lowered the knife slightly, his hand trembling with the tension.

'They asked for food, for help,' said Goldman, trying not to look at the man's disfigured face.

'We all need food here. Have you brought some? Where is it?'

'I have no food,' said Goldman. He paused. 'But I've brought money. For you.'

As he spoke the first drops of rain were beginning to fall. The man put the knife away inside his coat and pulled up the zip.

'Perhaps you should come and find shelter – and keep your money dry. It may shrink if it gets wet,' he said. Turning, he led Goldman into the camp. People looked up with interest as Goldman walked by. It was not often such a well-dressed person came their way.

The man stopped in front of a shack. He called out and a woman appeared. Goldman recognized her as the one who had been begging at the roadside.

'We have a guest,' said the man. 'He has brought money but he has no food. He cannot eat his money, so he will be our guest and eat with us.'

119

Inside the shack it was dark and cramped. Later, Goldman remembered being surprised that it did not smell. How did these people wash? How did they keep their homes so clean and tidy? Why did they bother in a place like this?

The woman placed a small bowl in front of Goldman and paused. 'I am sorry, but that is all we can offer you,' she said quietly. 'It is all we have.'

Goldman looked into the translucent liquid in which floated strands of what appeared to be grass. 'Thank you,' he said. He looked round the shack at the children. 'What about them?'

'They will eat later,' said the woman. 'You are our guest. It is our custom.'

There were no spoons, so Goldman and the father drank from the wooden bowls. The hot liquid tasted strange and Goldman struggled to swallow it down. 'What is it?' he asked eventually.

'Anything we can find,' said the younger man. 'Grass, leaves. But yesterday we found a rat. They have good nutrients.'

Goldman choked. 'How did you catch it?'

'The children found it,' said the man. 'It was dead.'

Goldman put down the bowl and rested his head in his hands, dizzy from the shock. After a few moments he raised his eyes and looked again at the children whose food he was eating. 'I can't do this. Please give it to them.'

The father nodded and took the bowl. The children approached the table eagerly. The rain spotted quietly on the rusted roof of the shack.

'I am so sorry,' said Goldman. 'But there is money. You will be able to eat. The children will be able to eat.'

He put his hand in his pocket and pulled out the handkerchief. The coins were hard on the bare wood of the table. He pushed them towards the father.

But instead of taking the coins, the man shook his head. 'It is too late. We cannot eat your money. And we do not sell what you wish to buy.'

'I do not want to buy anything,' said Goldman urgently. 'I want to help.'

'Help who? Us – or yourself?'

'What do you mean?'

'Are you saying you don't feel pain? Guilt, perhaps? Maybe you think that by giving money you will take away the fear of what you might be learning about yourself. But it will not work. We are not priests: we cannot give you absolution.'

'If not for yourself, take it for your children,' said Goldman desperately, as if imploring the man to take the money. 'Look at them, they need help.'

The man leaned forward. Goldman sensed the anger in him and felt afraid.

'Look at them?' asked the father. 'I do look at them. I see children I love more than life itself, and I see their death. They are dying. It is too late.'

'But your wife, the woman – we saw her begging for money only days ago.'

The man stared at him. 'Days ago? No, not days ago, my friend. Many weeks ago. Many months ago. But it does not matter. It is too late. There are some things that cannot be changed now. If you want to help others then you need to fish further upstream.'

'What do you mean?' said Goldman.

'In your own pool. Among your own kind. That is where you need to speak of helping people. Of humanity. Of justice. Here we are dying from the poison your world pours down on us day after day.'

The father was silent for a moment. Then he shook his head. 'I am sorry,' he said. 'That was unkind. I know you came to help, but it is too late. Out here we are so far from food.'

'So what happens?' said Goldman.

'We die. We watch our children die, and then we die.'

'But there must be something . . .' said Goldman desperately.

The father looked into Goldman's face. 'Sometimes there is an answer, but we would rather die,' he said quietly.

'What?' said Goldman.

The man was silent, pain twisting his face. The infected eye socket seemed to be weeping. Then he said, 'There are worse things.'

'What worse things?' asked Goldman. 'What can be worse than this?'

The man remained silent. His tears fell on to the makeshift table, darkening the wood. Finally he straightened up and looked at Goldman, an expression of complete calm on his face. 'We too will die,' he said. 'That is all.'

A child came up and stood at his side, pressing against his father, staring at Goldman with great dark eyes. Almost absent-mindedly, the father put his arm round the child and held him close.

Watching them, Goldman's thoughts went back to his own child. The baby he had never held: the boy he had never seen. A photograph he had torn up and thrown away. Here in the shack, the warmth of the father's love as he held the child was like a judgement. He felt a pang of sorrow – and perhaps envy. Why was he always an outsider? He sighed in silent regret at what he had lost.

The rain was louder on the tin roof and a trickle of water crept across the dirt floor of the shack. Far off, thunder crackled like distant gunfire. In the shack it was still. No one moved. Goldman looked down at the money on the table.

The father smiled sadly, shaking his head. 'It is too late, my friend. We cannot eat gold. We are already in the jaws of the beast. We are already dead.'

Goldman opened his mouth to speak, but the words died soundlessly. Outside the shack, he became aware of torrential rain, and running feet splashing through the mud. He got up and went to the doorway. He leaned against the wooden frame. He felt sick.

He looked back into the darkness of the shack. In the far corner a small child was lying clutching a rag of blue fabric as if for comfort; the child's skin was stretched tight across the jutting bones. A fly settled on its face.

'Forgive me,' he said to the man at the table. 'I did not think – I did not know you suffered in this way. That you lived like this. Foraging like animals. It's degrading.'

The father raised a hand as if to still his own words before they caught fire in the heat of his anger. Then he was calm again. 'You are mistaken,' he said quietly. 'We are not degraded and we are not animals. We are dying but we are still people of dignity. It is the oppressor who is less than human. It is he who is degraded by his actions. What will such a person tell his grandchildren in years to come? That there were good people here. A people of peace, living in a land they loved. But he came and turned that land into a desert. How proud will his grandchildren be of him?'

Outside the hut the air was heavy and humid. Goldman was struggling to breathe. 'I'm sorry,' he said at last. 'I'm so sorry. I know that is not enough, but it's all I can say. I have no other words.'

The father stood and walked across to Goldman. 'It is enough,' he said quietly. 'Your thoughts are spoken in your silence. When you have no words, then we hear your sorrow. You are one with us.'

Goldman felt a surge of warmth at the words. You are one with us. He could not remember anyone ever saying that to him before. In this, the most alien of places, he felt a strange gratitude. Almost a sense of belonging.

Outside the rain was coming down with a relentless force, hammering on the ground. Goldman was vaguely aware of something happening in the clearing.

There was an unnatural darkness outside the shack. The shadows had returned, but this time they were not silent. There was a low growl as if a large creature stirred in anger. A rumbling, distant at first, which came not through the air but through the ground itself. Goldman shuddered. He felt afraid. Then, far off, there was a piercing cry: 'It comes.'

In a moment the air was full of shouting as people ran out of their shacks. Children were scrambling out of the dry river bed like startled birds. Women were screaming, men yelling in desperation.

Then it broke over them. At first it was a fast-moving shadow rushing at them through the trees. Then a wall of foaming brown water burst through the undergrowth, curling and roaring, ripping up trees and bushes, tearing into the shacks and hurling old, rusted cars aside. Howling through the encampment in an avalanche of destruction.

Goldman ran but the torrent caught him and brought him down. For a moment he caught a glimpse of the sky through the brown water above him. There was a crushing pain in his chest. Then darkness.

He woke, choking on the foul water in his throat. Around him was devastation. The camp was gone. The torrent had subsided and there was silence except for the crying. People wandered round in a daze, searching for their possessions, their homes. Their children.

Goldman stood up shakily. He pulled off his sodden jacket, wringing it out to get rid of the water. Everything was covered in mud and filth. In the distance, along the side of the river, was a fleck of blue. He rubbed his eyes and walked unsteadily towards it. Then he stopped and cried out.

Near the scrap of cloth, almost buried in the mud, was the body of a child; a small arm reached up as if pleading for help.

Goldman walked slowly back along the riverbank. The woman was sitting by the ruins of her home, staring into her grief. He took his jacket and put it round her. His hands lingered for a moment on her thin shoulders. He felt her body shaking with the pain of all she had lost. In the mud at his feet, he saw the dull yellow of a coin.

He set off back to the road, walking in silence the way he had come. He thought of the desolation at the camp. Maybe he should have stopped to help. But help them do what? Bury their dead? Like the child whose body he had seen in the mud?

He imagined the child's last terrible moments as it was swept to its death in the foaming torrent. Tears ran down his face as he walked. It was as though he, too, was being swept along by a powerful current. Struggling, choking, drowning. Dying.

The high tower

It was almost nightfall when Goldman arrived back. Sheppard was watchful but did not question Goldman about his disappearance. They shared what remained of their food and then turned in for the night.

The next day the walking seemed unusually monotonous, despite their aching shoulders. They had been climbing steadily for several hours, but now the ground levelled off. Bushes and long grass obscured the view so that they felt as though they were walking through a long tunnel of undergrowth.

How they avoided disaster, they never knew. One moment they were trudging laboriously in single file, Sheppard leading, along the narrow path with bushes on either side. Then, without warning, the ground to their right suddenly collapsed, sweeping Sheppard's legs from under him. He cried out as the earth and bushes dropped away, leaving him clinging to the edge of a sheer drop of thirty feet or more. Goldman threw down his bags and rushed forward.

'Stay back,' yelled Sheppard. 'It's not safe.'

'Shut up and give me your hand,' replied Goldman grimly. 'If you go, we both go.'

As Goldman grabbed hold of his arms, he realized that the bag over Sheppard's shoulder was pulling him backwards. Goldman looked over the edge to the trees far beneath them and felt sickeningly dizzy. I can't do this, he thought. I've got to let him go.

Then the image of the squatter camp came into his mind. The father getting up from the table and walking over to him. What was it he had said? 'You are one with us.'

One with us. That's what he was. One with them: one with Sheppard.

'You're not bloody well going anywhere without me,' he yelled.

125

With a great shout he hauled on Sheppard's arms, struggling to pull him back, willing him back, to safety. At last, with a tremendous heave, he dragged him on to solid ground.

Sheppard lay groaning for several minutes as both men recovered from the shock. Eventually he said, 'Goldman, that was amazing. I don't know how you did that. Are you OK?'

'Never mind about me. How are you?' said Goldman. He was trembling with the exertion.

Sheppard got slowly to his feet and brushed the soil off his clothes. Gradually their fear began to subside and they could think more clearly. 'I didn't realize we were walking along a cliff edge,' he said. 'We'll have to make a detour.'

It took them a long time to force their way through the undergrowth before they thought it safe to rejoin the path. As they stopped for breath, Sheppard looked back at the route they had taken. 'You know, I'm not sure that was a cliff. It seems man-made to me.'

He pointed through a gap in the bushes. 'There,' he said. 'That's some sort of terracing. It's like a stadium. Look how it curves round. It's an outdoor amphitheatre.' He paused, then said, 'How do you feel about going down to have a look?'

'I'm not sure about that,' said Goldman doubtfully. 'It looks a long way down and my legs are tired. It'll take hours. You go if you want. I'm staying here.'

'Oh, come on, it won't take that long,' said Sheppard. 'It'll make a change from walking along this endless path. Anyway, I'd be quite interested to see where I'd have ended up if you hadn't come to the rescue.'

Goldman shrugged. 'Whatever you say.'

Despite Sheppard's reassurances, it took longer than they expected to make their way round to the terracing and scramble down the tiers of roughly hewn stonework. As they descended they found themselves dropping down out of the sunlight.

It was cold in the shadows. At each level the temperature seemed to fall, until they felt as though they were sinking into icy water. The base of the arena was overgrown, but standing there on what might have been a stage they could sense the drama of the ancient structure. Sheppard shivered.

'It's so cold here,' said Goldman.

'I was thinking of something else,' said Sheppard.

'What's on your mind?'

'Something a poet called Dante wrote, centuries ago.'

'More bad news?'

Sheppard nodded. Goldman was silent for a few moments, then said, 'Tell me.'

'You're a glutton for punishment.'

'Listen,' said Goldman, 'I've been drunk often enough to know that when you're on your knees puking into the toilet, it's all got to come up.'

'Is that what this feels like?'

Goldman shrugged. 'I don't know. It's what came into my head. All I know is that I can't run away any more.'

Sheppard sighed. 'OK, but don't say I didn't warn you. It's a poem about two men who travelled down into the depths of hell.'

'That sounds familiar,' said Goldman with grim humour.

'They climb down a series of stone terraces. As they go down, they encounter people who've done terrible things. At each level the crimes these people have committed, and their punishments, get worse.'

'And they're all being roasted alive?' said Goldman.

'Some are, yes. But as they go deeper and meet people who've done even worse things, it's the exact opposite. In the upper levels there is fire and heat, but further down it turns freezing cold. Until, at the bottom, there's solid ice.'

'And that's what made you shiver?'

'Partly – climbing down here reminded me of the story. But there was something else. The travellers found two of the most evil men, imprisoned up to their necks in the ice.' He paused.

'Tell me,' said Goldman uneasily.

'Well, the story is that, centuries ago, there was a war. There were two powerful men who were allies. One was called Count Ugolino and the other was an archbishop. After the fighting was over, the two men became rivals for power. The archbishop turned on Ugolino and locked him up with his children in a room at the top of a tower. Each day the guard brought the prisoners food. But one day, there was no food. Instead, Ugolino heard the sound of hammering at the base of the tower. The archbishop had nailed the door up.'

'Go on,' said Goldman.

'The count was faced with the prospect of watching his children starve to death in front of his eyes. Then one day, one of his children came to him and said, "Father, you gave us life. You must take that life back."'

There was horror on Goldman's face. 'What did he mean?'

'The child was offering his own body as food for the others,' said Sheppard. 'But the father could not do what the child asked.'

'So what happened then?' asked Goldman.

'They all starved to death.'

Goldman had a strange look on his face. At first he seemed incapable of speaking. Then he muttered, 'And they were in hell? The two evil men?'

Sheppard looked at Goldman. 'In the story, yes. Ugolino and the archbishop were in hell. They were stuck together in a hole in the frozen lake with just their heads and shoulders showing.'

Goldman turned away with a strange, high-pitched cry.

Sheppard said, 'I'm sorry. I suppose climbing down these tiers of stone seats reminded me. That and the cold down here.'

Goldman said nothing but set off, stumbling up the steep side of the amphitheatre as fast as he could.

Sheppard watched him struggling up the terracing, then set off after him. 'Hey, come on, it was only a story,' he called. Goldman did not reply.

They walked for a long time. Sheppard tried to make conversation but Goldman shook his head and walked on in silence, his eyes fixed on the ground.

It was evening before Sheppard could get him to speak.

'Look, I'm sorry about what happened back there,' said Sheppard. 'I didn't realize it would upset you like that.'

Goldman looked up. 'It's not just a story. It's real. It's what's going to happen to me. Maybe it's already happening.'

'What on earth do you mean?'

'You never asked where I went yesterday. I took some of the money and tried to find that woman who was begging. I found a squatter camp by a dried-out river bed. But then it all went wrong. It started raining – hard. There was a flash flood, or whatever they call it. Everything got swept away. The shacks – everything. Those people, the ones who were left, had nothing. No homes, no food – nothing. But, before the flood hit, I met a family. Those people were hungry, Sheppard. I mean really hungry.'

He hesitated. 'The father told me a story about another family who had also been starving to death . . .'

'And?'

'He said, "There are worse things." I didn't know what he meant. But that's it. That's what they were going to do. Like your story just now. The child was offering its own body as food for the others. I've just realized what the man was saying . . .'

Sheppard thought for a moment. 'Goldman, that's terrible, but it's not the same as the story. The archbishop murdered Ugolino and his children. But you're not the archbishop. Come on. It's OK.'

Goldman stared back, his eyes empty. 'No, you're wrong,' he said. 'You're so wrong.' He lay down on the grass, curling up like a foetus. Eventually his sobbing ceased, but he could not sleep.

Part 3

Fields of death

The next morning Sheppard awoke to hear Goldman muttering to himself. 'Is everything all right?' he asked.

Goldman turned and stared at him. 'No, it's not. We've been robbed. The money's gone.' He sat down on the grass, his head in his hands.

'All of it?' said Sheppard, sitting up and rubbing the sleep out of his eyes.

'The lot.'

There was silence. Then Sheppard said, 'You sound a bit strange. Are you angry with me? Do you think that I've taken it?'

Goldman looked at him for a moment. 'No, I don't think that. You aren't interested in money. In fact, I'm not sure I'm interested in the damned stuff any more. You never thought you'd hear me say that, did you? Well – it's true. And I'm not angry with you. I'm angry with myself.'

'There's something else, isn't there,' said Sheppard. 'Tell me.'

Goldman was silent for a long time. Then he said, 'You're right, there is something else. I was thinking about those people in the squatter camp. I couldn't get them out of my mind. I saw the bodies lying there. Some of them were children – a lot of them were children. The men were trying to bury them, but they had no spades or shovels. Just bare hands. How bad is that, when you can't afford a shovel to bury your kids, so all you can do is scrape mud over the bodies to keep the flies away? And it was my fault,' he said. 'I did that. Kicking people out of their homes, shoving people off their land to build new factories, gambling on commodities that screw up food prices and leave people to starve.'

Goldman paused, gathering strength to continue. 'Starve, Sheppard. I locked them up in a tower and threw away the bloody key. Well, now I've seen what it means. Those people were there, right in front of me. And all the time we were lugging around bags of money. More money than they could imagine. Money that could have helped them. Saved them. Last night I kept thinking about that kid, the one with the bit of blue rag. I wanted him to live. I don't know why, but it seemed the most important thing in the world. Then I found his body in the mud. He's dead.'

'The most important thing in the world?' said Sheppard, almost to himself. He had a faraway look on his face. He turned to Goldman. 'Why did you go back?'

Goldman was silent for a moment. 'I don't know. To try to change things. To help them. To do something – anything.'

Sheppard looked thoughtful.

'What?' said Goldman.

'I was wondering what those people valued more – your money or the fact that you went back.'

Nothing more was said about the missing money. It was almost as though Goldman had forgotten about it. By late afternoon they were tired out, even though they were no longer burdened by the heavy bags. They stopped to set up camp and Sheppard started clearing a patch of ground where they could sleep.

Goldman remained agitated. Finally he stood up and walked off into the trees.

* * *

As he walked it seemed to be getting warmer. Hotter. Ahead there were sounds, faint at first but growing louder. At last he emerged from among the trees – and into a nightmare. He held his hands to his ears but the sound pulsed through his skull. He shut his eyes tightly but the vision blazed more brightly.

Nothing had prepared him for this. As far as the eye could see, the earth was on fire. A sea of flame stretched to the distant horizon. It was as though the earth had been flayed alive, its skin peeled back to reveal a bloody, pulsing inferno beneath.

Shocked into immobility by the searing heat, Goldman could smell his clothes scorching. He put his hands to his eyes, but the image remained. Still it burned, white hot in some places but an ominous blood red in others.

For a moment Goldman thought he saw the outlines of shapes, perhaps figures, in a furnace. Further away, the flames darkened into deep slate before brightening once more at the horizon. The whole skyline was on fire, feathered like spray blown from wave crests, bleeding red into a blue-black sky. He looked up fearfully. The empty night towered endlessly upwards into a great cathedral of darkness.

Goldman stared, transfixed. Slowly now, the colours were beginning to change. Darkening, like a winter's afternoon. The earth grew cold. He shivered. Instead of the burning and the flames came ice, spreading silently across the landscape. In the distance, through the gathering gloom, he could see figures stooping, as though digging in the snow.

Goldman sensed a movement behind him. Turning, he saw Sheppard standing back among the trees. 'Who are they?' he asked.

Sheppard said nothing. He looked old and tired.

Goldman turned back. A hard layer of frozen snow crusted the ground. In the far distance, trees stood bare and black against the low cloud. The vast horizon made him shudder with a sense of isolation. The men digging in the frozen ground were tiny against the wide empty landscape. Lost in its silence.

As Goldman stared into the half-light, he thought he recognized some of those who were digging. Flickering images from old black-and-white newsreels came back to him.

One of the men stopped digging. Straightening up, he turned. Goldman was filled with fear and panic. It was a face he recognized. In his mind's eye he saw the news footage: the crowds shouting hysterically, arms raised in salute, and high up on the podium the figure of the leader. Then powerful and triumphant – now an old man with a shovel.

Further off was another familiar figure: stocky, with a heavy moustache. Was this old man the monster who murdered millions of his own countrymen?

In the distance were others. As the figures dug silently in the cold earth, Goldman sensed an aura – not of bitterness and resentment, but something else. From time to time one of the figures would stop digging and kneel in the snow as at a graveside. Words were spoken; something rose up from the earth. An embrace, a cry. Of pain? Goldman was not sure. He felt faint. He turned, but Sheppard had disappeared.

Goldman set off slowly back to the camp. He had not gone far when he began to feel cold, as though he was walking through a freezing fog. His feet were icy. He quickened his pace, but the cold was spreading slowly up his body.

He stopped. It was like standing in freezing water. The cold was moving up through his chest and into his throat. He began to choke. He leaned against a tree and tried to think. What was happening? Where was Sheppard?

He thought back to the fields of ice and the mysterious figures digging in the frozen earth. Goldman began to weep. He turned and rammed his forehead hard against the rough bark of the tree, impervious to the pain. Who were those men? Those who had caused so many deaths?

Goldman remembered others who had been killed. Victims of a different violence. Where was his shovel and where were his graves?

'Come away,' said a familiar voice behind him. He turned to see that Sheppard had returned.

'I was almost glad when I saw them out there,' whispered Goldman. 'Glad that there are men worse than me. Whoever they were. They killed millions and now they're being punished. But then I thought of the others. The ones I've killed. I'm as guilty as them. As damned as they are. Where are my graves? Where are my dead?'

'This is not for you,' said Sheppard softly. 'And it may not be what you think. You have your own task, your own choice. Your own burden. That is enough. Come away, my friend.'

Goldman followed him in silence like a small child. The coldness seemed to be receding. He could feel his feet again. Eventually they reached camp and sat down.

'What was that?' said Goldman. 'A vision of hell? Are they condemned to dig up the bodies of their victims for ever? And why? To free them? I saw one rise up from the ground and reach out to the one who dug. What was that, Sheppard? What was that?' Tears were running down his face.

'You need some sleep,' said Sheppard. 'You're tired out.'

'How can I sleep?' said Goldman. 'I'll never sleep again.'

Sheppard came over and knelt beside him. He put an arm round Goldman's shoulder. 'Let it be for now,' he said. 'Let it be.'

The tree

Sheppard woke with a start. Something was wrong. The sun was already high in the sky. It was late – too late. He turned to Goldman, but he was gone.

Sheppard scrambled to his feet, his back and legs stiff from sleeping on the damp ground. He looked round but there was no sign of the other man. He cried out: 'Goldman! Goldman!' But there was no reply.

It took Sheppard several minutes to pick up the tracks. The grass was trodden and bruised by Goldman's stumbling feet. Sheppard followed the trail, calling all the time, but the sound echoed back in the silent woodland.

A veil of mist was beginning to creep slowly across the sun. It was cooler now in the thick undergrowth and Sheppard's shirt was cold with sweat against his body. He stopped to think. Even though he had lost the trail, there seemed no other route Goldman could have taken. Sheppard bent down and rubbed his aching ankles. He had forgotten to bring his stick.

As he straightened up, a thought struck him. No, not a thought: a song. A voice singing so quietly he could hardly hear it. He set off walking again. The mist was thicker now. He could hardly see his way through the trees.

Suddenly he held his breath. From somewhere, deep in the woods, there had been a sound. He listened intently. It came again. Despite the blanket of mist, it was unmistakeable. An animal in pain.

Sheppard plunged ahead, stumbling wildly through the under-growth until at last he came to a clearing. Then, through the fog, he saw it.

Goldman's body was hanging from a tree branch, turning slowly in the cold air. The mist seemed to drape it like a shroud.

For a moment there was silence, full of loneliness and despair. Then Sheppard ran forward, yelling to Goldman. He was hanging by his neck from the strip of coloured silk that had once been his tie. His tongue protruded grotesquely from his mouth. His eyes bulged, so that it seemed they would burst from their sockets.

Sheppard grabbed Goldman's ankles, trying to take the weight of the body. There was a groan. 'The tie! Unfasten it!' shouted Sheppard, struggling to support Goldman's body.

Goldman clawed at his throat, then let his arms fall to his sides. 'Can't,' he muttered through clenched teeth. 'Too tight.'

Sheppard released his hold. There was a terrible choking cry from Goldman as his neck took the full weight of his body again. Sheppard stepped back and looked up at Goldman's anguished face. He saw that he had fastened his belt round the tree branch, then threaded his tie through the loop of the belt to make the noose.

Sheppard ran, limping, over to the trunk of the tree and started to climb. His shoes slipped on the wet bark as he tried to get a foothold. It was several minutes before he was able to crawl slowly out on to the branch where Goldman was hanging. He pulled frantically on the belt to loosen it. Each time he pulled on the strap, Goldman groaned.

Then, without warning, the belt came free. Goldman crashed to the ground. He lay, not moving, as Sheppard scrambled back down the tree. He pulled the silk noose from Goldman's neck and held him in his arms, rocking him like a mother with an injured child.

Goldman sobbed. Sheppard could feel his body shaking.

Goldman was silent for a long time, clutching his neck where the skin had been rubbed raw by the tie.

'Why did you do that?' asked Sheppard eventually, his voice hardly more than a whisper.

'No good,' muttered Goldman. 'No good. Too much bad stuff. Deaths. The pain I caused. All of it. I wanted to die.'

He looked up at Sheppard as if expecting his companion to strike him.

'I don't think that's an option now,' said Sheppard.

'So this is it?' said Goldman slowly. 'Condemned to live with the past? With no escape?'

Sheppard shrugged.

Goldman looked up at Sheppard, his eyes empty. 'Why did you come looking for me?'

Sheppard said nothing, letting Goldman's words settle into the silence. Then he asked, 'Do you think you'll be able to walk? We need to get away from here. Let's try to keep moving. You know what they say. Don't look back. Don't look down.'

Goldman raised a hand to his face as though feeling tentatively for something. Then he let his hand fall back at his side. 'Don't look back. Don't look anywhere,' he said quietly. 'That's the trouble. Something's happened to my eyes. I can't see anything.'

'What are you talking about?'

'My eyes. Something's wrong with them. I think I've gone blind.'

'What?'

'I'm telling you – I can't see anything. What am I going to do?'

'Well, whatever happens, we're going to stick together,' said Sheppard unconvincingly.

'I think it was the light,' said Goldman.

'What do you mean? What light?'

'Up there,' said Goldman quietly. 'Tying the belt on the branch. And then – falling. I didn't jump, Sheppard, I fell.'

Sheppard was silent.

'It was like slow motion,' said Goldman. 'But then something happened. It was as though someone caught me. Just as the cord was jerking tight round my neck.'

'Who was it who caught you?' said Sheppard.

'I don't know. The sun was shining in my eyes and dazzling me. There was something there. Holding me. And singing. A very quiet singing in my head. It held me until you came.'

'Maybe it was the shock,' said Sheppard. 'The trauma. It could be your mind trying to cope with what you've been through.'

Goldman shrugged. 'Maybe you're right. But – '

'But what?' said Sheppard.

'Nothing.'

It took them a long time to struggle back to the path. Several times they got lost and found themselves back where they started. It was beginning to get dark.

Goldman was unable to walk unaided, so Sheppard had to half-carry him through the dense undergrowth. By the time they reached the clearing they were utterly exhausted.

'Are you there?' said Goldman anxiously.

'Yes, don't worry, I'm here. How are you feeling?' He sensed that a great emptiness had come over the other man.

Goldman shook his head but said nothing.

'What is it, Goldman? Tell me.'

'Last night I had another of those dreams,' Goldman said. 'Nightmares. I dreamed that I was back in that pub. The place where we stayed early on.' He paused. 'You remember that young woman? The one I slept with? I dreamed about her. About what happened. Except that in the dream I realized who she was.'

'And who was she?' said Sheppard.

Goldman's unseeing eyes were full of tears. At first he could not speak. Then, very quietly, he said, 'She was my sister.'

'In your dream she may have been your sister, Goldman. But only in your dream.'

'No. She really was my sister. When we were in the pub she seemed familiar. As though we had met before. As though I knew her. Maybe that's why she was so keen to talk to me. That's what she wanted – to talk to me. That's all. It was real. It wasn't just that she looked familiar, it was her. Then I thought about what you said: how she must have needed the money very badly to sleep with someone like me. I thought about that night – and about all the other nights. All the other women I'd had in the past. The women people had arranged for me. Young women like the one in the hospice. The one who had her face slashed by the pimp. It was as though they were all my sister. And I wondered what she must be thinking of me. In the dream she reached out and touched my hand. She said something, but I couldn't hear the words. I could never hear the words. All I could think of was what I had done to her. Disfigured her. And then I woke up.'

'It was a dream, Goldman.'

'Was it? I don't think so. Because when I woke, the dream hadn't stopped. It won't ever stop. It was her. It's as though all the things I have done, I have done to her. I couldn't bear that. So I went away. As far away as I could go. And that's it. That's how it ends, Sheppard. Trapped in this mess for ever. All the time my options are shutting down – and now my eyes. If I can't see, how am I ever going to find my way back to fetch my things? And if I ever do manage to fetch my things, how can I bear to be who I am?'

'It's bad, I agree,' admitted Sheppard. 'But we have to press on. We need to get back to the river.'

'Why?' said Goldman. 'We've lost the money so we need to go back to Tresco and get more things, don't we?'

'Do you really think we can make it all that way back to the house?'

After a pause, Goldman said, 'No, you're right. We're stuffed.'

'Not quite,' said Sheppard. 'We need to get back to the river, and then take stock. Maybe talk to Raffa about it. For now we've got to keep walking – and keep hoping.'

'There is no hope,' said Goldman in a whisper.

'That's when we have to keep hoping,' said Sheppard.

The reckoning

They were a strange sight. Like two grotesque figures from a panto-mime or a carnival: Sheppard walking in front and, connected by the stick, Goldman following behind. Every few yards Sheppard would call out a warning: 'Low branch. Path uneven. Steep climb coming up.'

Goldman found it easier to grip his end of the stick with both hands, which gave him the strange appearance of a penitent at prayer.

At one point Sheppard stopped. 'I'm sorry to have to walk in front all the time,' he said, 'but I'm not sure what alternative there is.'

'The lame leading the blind,' replied Goldman. 'It doesn't matter anyway – you've been leading me ever since we set out on this journey.'

Sheppard did not reply. Without the support of the stick, his ankles were causing him increasing pain. He was limping badly and Goldman sensed the painful unevenness of step through the stick.

'How are you doing?' he said.

'I'm managing,' replied Sheppard. 'How about you?'

'I'm OK,' said Goldman.

They walked in this tandem fashion for two days, possibly three. Then, one morning after they had been walking for over an hour, Goldman stopped, jerking Sheppard to a halt.

'What's wrong?' said Sheppard, turning.

Goldman let go of the stick and stood with his arms at his side, his face calm. 'It's over,' he said.

'What is?'

'Walking – this journey. All this time I've been fretting about how to get my stuff to the river. But it's not going to happen. I'll never do it. I'm going to be here for ever trying to find my way. Carrying bits of my stuff, if I can find it. Raphael said I needed to bring all my things. But some of the money got lost in the sea – and then other bits got given away. Then the bags disappeared. It's hopeless. And don't think about helping me: it's not your job. You've helped me already. You've helped me see the mess I've made of things. The suffering, the deaths. I'm finished. And there's no one to blame but myself.'

'I'm sorry,' said Sheppard. 'I'm not sure what to say. We need a break. I could do with a breather.'

'It's OK,' said Goldman. 'I've finally worked it out. I don't belong over there – on the other side of the river. I belong here, in the dark. I'm not fit to go across. Do you know what I mean?'

'I hear what you're saying,' said Sheppard, 'but I'm not sure I agree with you. Let's keep moving and see what happens when we get to the river. It can't be far off now.'

'Don't try to cheer me up,' said Goldman. 'I'm OK about this. It's what needs to be. This is the bottom line and it says bankrupt. Busted. Finished. Damned by my own greed and stupidity. How long do you think it will take for my clothes to wear out, my shoes to drop to bits? And there I'd be, blind and naked as a rat, struggling through these woods trying to find all my stuff. Lost for all eternity. And you think that's the worst that can happen? Well, it's not. It may sound like hell, but it isn't. I'll tell you what hell is, Sheppard. Hell is to do all that, to walk all those miles and carry all that stuff – while all the time loathing the very things you once fought for. Things I was so proud of. Things that now seem such an obscenity I can hardly bear to think of them. If we ever get back to Raphael, I'm going to tell him it's not going to work. Tell him I'm finished. Stay over here. Hide away. Anything.'

'Maybe we're getting near the end of the journey,' Sheppard said.

Goldman seemed not to have heard him and they set off once more, stumbling over the rough ground like drunken men: Sheppard limping badly, Goldman dragging on the stick, a dead weight.

Then, finally, when they felt too exhausted to walk another stumbling, agonizing step, far ahead Sheppard glimpsed the river and a familiar figure.

* * *

Raphael glanced up. Catching sight of the two men through the trees, he waved and ran towards them.

Goldman felt Sheppard slow. 'What's happening?' he called out. 'Is there trouble?'

'No,' replied Sheppard. 'It's Raffa. We're there. We made it.'

Goldman dropped the stick. He could hear Raphael panting with the unaccustomed exertion. Then he heard his familiar voice. 'Welcome back. It's so good to see you both again.'

Goldman felt his hand being shaken vigorously, but he recoiled from the warmth of Raphael's greeting.

'Is something wrong?' asked Raffa. 'Was I too effusive in my welcome? I do apologize.'

Goldman said nothing. The three walked back towards the river, Goldman clinging to Sheppard's arm. He felt the ground gently dropping away as they got nearer the water.

They stopped and Goldman held out his hand, trying to locate Raphael. 'Raffa,' he said, 'I've got to talk to you. It's important. This journey – it's all gone wrong. The money's disappeared, and there's something else. I'm not going over to the other side. Not ever. There's been stuff that's happened. People we've met. Things I've realized. I'm tired. I can't do this any more. And, on top of all that, my eyes have stopped working. I'm blind, Raffa. I can't see.'

He paused, his arms outstretched as though in entreaty. The open palms were filthy. 'Raffa, are you there? Listen to me. I'm done for. Finished. I don't want to go across the river. Apart from anything else, I'm too ashamed.' His arms fell to his sides in despair. He sank to his knees in the dust and fell forward on all fours like a beaten animal.

'There is no need . . .' Raphael began. 'Do please stand up.'

Goldman was sobbing now. 'No! No! This is where I belong. This is who I am. A monster. I have done monstrous things.'

'Mr Goldman,' said Raphael, 'please stand up, you make me quite uncomfortable. I understand your feelings, but you may not be in possession of all the facts. Things may not be as they appear. In fact, I think you've been kept in the dark long enough.'

As he was speaking, a child walked quietly up to the three men. He stood staring gravely at the strange, crouching animal that was Goldman. Goldman felt a small hand touch his shoulder. Slowly the pain receded and he felt strangely peaceful. He got uncertainly to his feet and found himself being led down a shallow incline. In the quietness he could hear the gentle flowing of the river.

He felt the child tug gently on his arm and Goldman slowly lowered himself to his knees. His whole body was shaking.

There was the quiet scraping of pebbles being moved in wet gravel. Small fingers touched his face. Wet sand was being smeared on his eyelids. Its touch was rough on the sensitive skin. For a moment everything was still. Then cold water. A cloth wiping his eyes and face. The water was refreshing.

There was a silence, as though people were waiting for him to do something. He opened his eyes. Gradually his vision cleared and he saw standing in front of him a small boy holding a scrap of blue cloth. The child laughed at Goldman's surprise.

Goldman looked round for Sheppard and Raphael. Slowly the two figures came into focus. 'I can see,' he said quietly. 'Dear God, I can see.'

Raphael walked over. 'Mr Goldman, I am so pleased. I thought your problem would be temporary, but you can never be quite sure.'

Goldman looked at the small boy, still standing in front of him. 'Thank you,' he said. The boy laughed again and ran off, seemingly delighted.

'Raphael,' said Goldman, 'we need to talk. I don't know what's going on but I just wondered whether . . .' He paused. 'If my eyes are really OK, perhaps I could make myself useful round here. On this side of the river?'

Raphael shook his head. 'Thank you, Mr Goldman, but no. It's a kind offer, and one we don't receive very often, but I have something very important to tell you. You are cleared to cross the river. It's down here on my sheet in black and white.'

'But I'm not going across,' insisted Goldman. 'I've had enough of trying to carry all my stuff. Anyway, most of the money got stolen, and the rest of it got lost.'

Raphael looked uncomfortable, like a child who has been caught out. 'Mr Goldman, I owe you an apology. For the money that was, er, stolen. I'm afraid that was my fault. It happened that I was passing your way and thought you might appreciate a hand. So I brought it on ahead. I should have left a note but I must have forgotten. I'm so sorry if I've caused you more distress.'

Goldman looked uncertain. 'But there's all the rest of my things. What I'm saying is I'm not going back. I don't give a damn about the rest of it.'

Raphael raised an eyebrow. 'But you made it very clear at the outset that your possessions were of great importance to you. You particularly wanted to have all your things with you. The things that make you what you are. I wrote your words down very carefully.'

'Well, that may have been true then, but it's not now,' said Goldman. 'I don't care if I never see that stuff again. In fact, I can't bear the thought of all the crap I've left back there.'

Raphael looked startled. 'Really?'

'Really,' said Goldman emphatically. 'I don't know what the hell was wrong with me. It was as though I was addicted to money and all the rest of the stuff. Like an alcoholic, always craving more booze. Pathetic – sick – that's what it was.'

'Well, perhaps that would explain why your transit papers have come through so quickly.' He glanced up at Goldman's look of incomprehension. 'The fact that you are cleared to go across the river,' said Raphael.

'But what about my stuff?' repeated Goldman, confused.

'Have you left behind anything at all of value?' asked Raphael.

Goldman was silent for a moment. 'No. There's nothing. Not a thing.'

'I thought that might be the case,' said Raphael. 'I could tell from your hands.'

'What about my hands?'

'When you were here before, your hands were clenched tight, holding on to everything that you had. Now your hands are open. You've let go.'

'And you don't need all my stuff?'

Raphael sighed. 'Mr Goldman, with great respect, we would prefer it if the place were not cluttered up with your possessions. All we are concerned about is you. Since you seem to have detached yourself from the things you accumulated over your life, there seems to be nothing stopping you walking across the stepping stones. Be assured, you'll find a warm welcome there.'

'And what about Sheppard?' said Goldman.

'Mr Sheppard may follow a little later. I understand he has one or two matters to attend to over here.'

Sheppard was smiling at Goldman's confusion. 'It's fine,' he said. 'Just go.'

'But there are things I wanted to ask Raffa,' said Goldman. 'About what's happened. About what I am. Maybe I could go across tomorrow?' he added hopefully. 'Please – it's really important.'

Raphael pursed his lips. 'This is very unusual,' he said. 'Most people are only too happy to cross over the river. But I have to admit, there's nothing in the regulations that says you have to leave immediately. Perhaps the best thing would be for you to get some sleep, and we can have a further conversation in the morning. But then you must go, Mr Goldman.'

Burning questions

Raphael woke first and was clearly in a businesslike mood. 'Time to make a start,' he said briskly when Sheppard and Goldman finally stirred.

Goldman was still reluctant to move on, as though he had become comfortable in the strange friendship that had developed with Sheppard. 'Listen, Raffa,' he said, 'those things I wanted to ask about. About the stuff that's happened to us.'

Raphael looked at his watch with a slight frown. 'Very well. What is it you wish to know?'

'For a start I want to know about the graves – the ones the condemned men are forced to dig. What was going on back there? And why is it that I'm not being made to open the graves of the people whose deaths I caused?'

Raphael looked pensive. 'Sit down for a moment, Mr Goldman. Let me try to explain. The men you saw, or think you saw, weren't forced to do anything. Whatever they might have been doing, they chose to do it. When they arrived here they each found themselves confronted by something even greater than the evil they had committed. What they encountered is a love so deep that it enfolds the terrible things they have done. As though it absorbs their evil deeds. What those men were required to bring with them when they came here was simply an acknowledgement of the truth. To face the reality of what they had done.'

'But wasn't that their punishment?' said Goldman, interrupting. 'To open up the graves of those whose lives they'd destroyed and to release their victims?'

'Perhaps there is no punishment, in your sense of the word,' said Raphael. He thought for a moment. 'It's strange how people always seem to want retribution. But that's not quite how it works. And as to meeting their victims, yes, they certainly do meet them, but they find that the vicious cycle of evil is reversed. You may think it's a soft option, but I'm not so sure. The past can't be rewritten or washed away. They are who they are. What they discover is that others are not the enemies they thought they were. So why, you ask, were they opening the graves? You'll find that they dig them willingly and gladly – that is, if they dig them at all.'

Goldman thought back to the fields of death and shuddered. 'What happens when the body is revealed?' he asked quietly.

'It is revealed as it truly is: a living person who greets its old adversary with love and forgiveness. As you have heard, there is a great pain in that, but it's the pain of healing.'

'Will they dig for ever?' asked Goldman, feeling light-headed. He suddenly recalled a hot summer's day in a school assembly when he had fainted.

Raffa waited for Goldman to focus again before he replied. 'What is for ever?' he said. 'How long have you and Sheppard been on the road? Months, years – or for just a moment? Eternity is no time at all. It is simply now.'

'So they've been let off?' said Goldman. 'Men who killed millions of innocent people? Don't things like the Holocaust count any more?'

Raphael smiled. 'Are numbers so important? I hope not. We're not accountants here. We don't keep a score of wrongs. But, since you raise the question, let's look at some of the figures. How many people did Hitler kill? Six million Jews? And another five or six million people the world tends to forget? And what about all the other holocausts? Countless more have died, and are still dying, from hunger and the greed of wealthy nations. What should we do – have a league table of evil?' He paused. 'Be careful how you answer that, Mr Goldman. Perhaps we should be cautious where we lay blame and attribute evil. For example, were men like Hitler born monsters? Or was what they became a result, at least in part, of what had happened to them and to their people?'

'So what was their version of events?' said Goldman.

Raphael shrugged. 'Why don't you ask someone who was there?'

'With him and the others?' said Goldman in alarm.

'Why not?' said Raphael. 'They are simply people with human failings like everyone else. Nothing more, nothing less. You can speak to one of them as easily as you speak to Sheppard. Try to overcome your fear. He may be able to help you to reflect on your own circumstances.'

Engrossed in the conversation, Goldman had not noticed a solitary figure walking towards them. As the man came closer, Goldman asked, 'Who is that?'

'His name is Gruber,' said Raphael quietly, 'and he is loved. You have much in common.'

The white-haired man held out his hand. Goldman felt a familiarity – as though they had met before. The handshake was firm but Goldman found himself instinctively pulling away from physical contact.

'I know,' said the man. 'It is hard to touch one of those the world hates.'

Goldman noticed that the man had a slight German accent. They sat down. Goldman felt uncomfortable – vulnerable.

'Let me tell you how it was,' Gruber said. 'Or, at least, how it seemed. I was a soldier. Patriotic. Some said brave. My country was fighting a war, and we were winning. Then America entered the conflict, and before we knew it, all was lost. We were defeated and humiliated. I myself was badly wounded. A few years later there was an economic crisis in America – you call it the Crash? Its effects were felt across the world. After our military defeat came economic ruin. People starved to death in the streets. Men and women. Even our children. We believed ourselves to be the victims of a terrible injustice. There was unspeakable suffering among our people. And with it came a burning anger. So we – a group of us – swore that we would restore the honour of our nation. We would never again be defeated. We would put right the injustice we had suffered. We began to build a new political party. One based on absolute discipline. We would be ruthless in our quest for power and honour. We would build a new nation, one that would last a thousand years.'

He frowned and was silent for a moment before continuing so quietly that Goldman could hardly hear him.

'Sometimes, when people are oppressed, they turn on each other. As if that is the only way they can express their anger and frustration. So it was with us. We turned on our own people. The madness started slowly. Almost unnoticed at first. Like an infection. Then faster and faster, until it possessed us all.'

'But didn't you realize what was going on?' said Goldman, speaking for the first time. He was afraid that his question would unleash a torrent of anger.

'Yes,' said Gruber softly. 'Some of us did. But we pretended it was not so. We were running before an avalanche of our own making. There seemed no escape.'

'And did no one try to stop it?' said Goldman.

'Oh yes, many people. Thousands of them. Brave people who could see where the madness was leading. But we were too strong for them. Too well organized. Once there was a bomb, an assassination plot, but we escaped. It would have been better if they had succeeded, I think.'

'And is that it? said Goldman.

Gruber shook his head. 'No, there is more, my friend. There is death. We humans are born with the greatest gifts imaginable – self-awareness and intelligence. We try to control our own lives and the world around us. But there is also a shadow: some call it a curse. It is the knowledge that, one day, we will die – and life, in all its richness, will be obliterated. It is the fear that, finally, no matter who we are, we will cease to be. Death walks beside us every step of the way, mocking our hopes and dreams.'

'But what has that to do with the things you did?' said Goldman.

Gruber carried on speaking as though he had not heard the question. 'Some people respond to the curse with charity and love. Some withdraw into denial. But some, like you and me, respond with anger.

We loot and kill and that gives us the satisfaction of knowing that, as others die, we are still alive. We still have power and, we foolishly believe, control. Why else did you build your business empire? Because you were afraid. Afraid of being unnoticed. Of disappearing. Why did we do those things? Because we, too, lived in fear.'

After a pause, the man stood and held out his hand in parting. 'Go well, my brother. Remember me when you cross the river.'

'Are you not going over?' said Goldman.

'Not yet,' said the other. 'I could not bear the pain.'

'Of your punishment?'

'Of my forgiveness.' He paused for a moment. 'Or perhaps of something else.'

'Who are you?' said Goldman.

'Like you. One who has been given life.'

As he walked away, Goldman felt overwhelmed with sadness. He turned back to Raphael. Suddenly he clutched his head and cried out in pain. It felt as though his brain was bursting out of his skull.

Raphael smiled. He put an arm round him. 'Yes, it hurts, but only for an instant. Then it is gone. The pain is simply your fear pulling away from you. The monster in the woods – that thing that frightened you so much – was very real. You were right, it was a predatory monster, and in a way it was trying to harm you. But it was not external; that's why Sheppard couldn't see or hear it. It was your fear, trying to drag you back into your past. It was the shadow of who you really are. But you are free now. You are yourself.'

'And the people whose deaths I caused?' said Goldman. 'Will I have to face them? What sort of freedom is that?'

Raphael was silent for a moment. 'Don't worry. You have already met many of them on your travels and you will meet more. When that happens, you'll find you are welcomed, not condemned. That is your freedom. Trust me. When you meet the people you have wronged, you'll find that they don't hate you or want revenge for what they suffered. And why not? Because they will recognize you not as their enemy, but as a friend. They won't forget what happened, and neither will you. But the pain will have gone and something more important will have become part of you both.'

'What's that?' said Goldman.

'Things that so many people ridicule, but which are at the heart of life: gratitude, forgiveness – love.'

'But how can I be forgiven for all the things I did?'

Raffa chuckled thoughtfully.

'What's so funny about that?' demanded Goldman.

'Because, in a strange way, forgiveness hardly matters.'

'It's all that matters,' protested Goldman. 'I realize that now.'

'Really?' said Raffa. 'Let me tell you a story. Once there was a little girl, perhaps five years old. One day her mother gave her a drink of fruit juice. "Be careful not to spill it," she said. But the little girl was distracted by other things and somehow the drink got knocked over – staining their new carpet. In horror the child ran out of the house. All day and all night they searched for her. The mother was out of her mind with worry. On the second night it was raining and the little girl was still missing. The mother sat up in her dressing gown, hoping and praying her daughter had come to no harm. Suddenly, the phone rang. It was the police. The girl had been found safe and well. She was on her way home in a police car. So, what do you think the mother did?' asked Raffa. 'Did she sit down and consider whether or not she would forgive the child for spilling the drink on the carpet? No. Still in her nightdress and slippers, she dashed out of the house and ran down the street in the pouring rain. She threw her arms round her child and wept for joy. Forgiveness was the last thing on her mind.'

Raffa grinned. 'And did they go out and buy another carpet?' he continued. 'No. The mother decided that she would keep the carpet with the stain on it as a reminder of how much she loved the child she had feared was dead.'

Goldman looked doubtful.

'You don't have to take my word for it,' said Raphael, laughing. 'You'll find out for yourself.'

The two men stood up. Raphael put his hand on Goldman's shoulder. 'It's been good meeting again, but now it is time for you to go. If you have more questions, you'll meet lots of people better informed than I.'

As Goldman turned to leave, he paused. 'The old man – Gruber. That wasn't his real name, was it?'

Raphael smiled. 'It is of no consequence. What matters is that he is loved.'

Surprise encounters

Goldman turned to Sheppard. 'Is this goodbye, then?'

'For the time being, perhaps, but we'll probably bump into each other again.' The two shook hands, then burst out laughing and hugged each other.

Sheppard put an arm affectionately round Goldman's shoulders. 'It's time to be on your way. And it looks as though you'll have company on the next part of your journey.'

Goldman looked towards the river. The small child with the scrap of blue cloth was standing by the stepping stones. 'I don't want to go,' said Goldman, suddenly afraid. 'I won't know anybody over there.'

'Just go,' said Sheppard gently. 'It'll be fine – it really will. You'll see.'

The two travellers embraced again, and Goldman walked reluctantly down to the water's edge. The small child grinned and, turning, stepped out on to the first of the flat stones that stretched across the slow-moving water.

Goldman followed, apprehensive in case he slipped. At the second stepping stone he almost stumbled. The stones seemed wider apart now and the water faster moving. He glanced up to see where the child was. As he looked across the stones ahead of him, the child was taller than Goldman remembered.

Ahead was the other riverbank. He thought back to Rosie's boat and the surf on the distant shore. Maybe everything was going to work out after all.

At the fourth stone he stopped again. The child had paused to tie the blue rag round his head like a sweatband. He turned back and waved encouragingly. Goldman saw that he was no longer a child but a strongly built young man.

The youth laughed at Goldman's surprise. 'Come on,' he shouted. 'Things to do. People to meet!' His voice was not that of a boy, but of a man. He turned and ran across the last of the stepping stones and on to the riverbank with the power and grace of a dancer.

Goldman could hear his laughter. For some reason his mind went back to Trudi and their brief marriage. A vague and distant memory – something about the way she had moved. That same lightness of step.

Alone now, Goldman faltered, then stopped. He realized how dirty he was. His trousers were mud-stained and his shirt was filthy. He felt stupid.

This is wrong, he thought. I don't belong over there. It's a mistake. They'll laugh at me. No, they won't – they'll hate me. He felt like a frightened little boy ushered into a room of strangers at a children's party.

As he came to the last stepping stone, he missed his footing. There was a stab of pain as his shin grazed the stone and he found himself standing awkwardly with one leg in the water. His trouser leg was soaking wet up to the knee and there was a tear in the cloth. He felt humiliated – ridiculous.

He looked back at Sheppard helplessly. 'I can't do this,' he shouted, angry with himself. 'I'm coming back.'

'No – keep going,' yelled Sheppard. 'You're almost there.'

That's just the problem, thought Goldman. I don't want to be there.

As he stepped on to the far bank of the river, he saw to his relief that the place was deserted. There was not a soul in sight. In the distance to his right he could hear the heavy beat of music and he walked hesitantly along the riverbank towards it.

Suddenly, it was as though he had passed through an invisible wall. The sound was deafening. He found that he was standing at the back of a huge crowd of people all yelling and waving crazily at a group pumping out thunderous rock music.

At the edge of the crowd, just in front of Goldman, a tall man dressed in blue and a young woman in jeans and a sweat-stained

T-shirt were both jumping up and down wildly. At the woman's feet was a coil of yellow climbing rope.

As the music came to an end with an ear-splitting crescendo, the crowd erupted in applause. The man turned. His face was proud, with a hooked nose. It looked like a face from an ancient Roman coin. When he saw Goldman, the man flung out his arms enthusiastically. 'Magnifico, magnifico,' he shouted in a strong Italian accent. 'Molto, molto bene.'

He turned and walked off, beaming. Then, abruptly, he stopped, as though he had thought of something. He walked back to Goldman and clutched his hand. 'I sorry,' he shouted over the noise of the crowd. 'Very sorry. Ugolino story not good. I sorry it give you bad time. The ice. Was no ice.' He stepped forward and kissed Goldman urgently on both cheeks. 'Please. You forgive me.'

He walked away. Goldman felt dazed.

Meanwhile the woman in the T-shirt and jeans was still jumping up and down with excitement as the applause continued. Without warning, she caught her heel in the coil of rope at her feet and tumbled backwards on the ground. As Goldman stepped forward to help, he found himself looking into her face. She looked familiar.

'That was very good timing, Harry,' she said.

Goldman felt that he knew her but, for a moment, could not remember who she was. Then he knew. At home as a child: on the shelf over the fireplace, a wedding photograph. A young woman smiling out at him. The same face that was smiling up at him now.

'Don't you know me?' she said, scrambling to her feet.

'Mother?' said Goldman, stunned.

The young woman put her arms round him and held him for a long time.

'Is it really you?' he said eventually. 'I can't get my mind round all this. And, anyway, what's that rope for?'

'Rock climbing,' she said, hitching the coil of rope over her shoulder. 'I'm quite good. You should try it some time.'

'But you're scared of heights,' said Goldman.

'That was before. It's different now. One of the things I left behind at the river was my fear.'

She laughed at Goldman's confusion. 'I know, it's not what I expected either. I thought I'd be bored to death, but I've never been so excited in my life. There's so much to do. So much to learn. I've made friends with a poet. He was here with me a minute ago. He's teaching me Italian. Look, he's over there, talking to that young woman. Dorothy. She's a writer, too. When I was younger, I never had the chance to do things like this, but I'm making up for it now.'

Goldman frowned. 'But I thought it would be –'

'Serene? Pink clouds? Forget it. It's busy and sometimes it gets pretty rowdy, as you'll have gathered. This place is great.'

As she spoke a large, bearded man carrying a guitar came ambling past. 'Hey,' he said, giving Goldman a playful punch on the shoulder. 'Good to see you, man. Sorry you missed the gig; we were expecting you yesterday. We'll do it again sometime, yeh?'

Goldman noticed that his arms were covered in tattoos. As he walked away, Goldman's mother said, 'They're noisy, but they're good boys.'

'I don't belong here,' said Goldman, embarrassed. 'There's been a misunderstanding.'

'No, there hasn't, Harry. Listen to me. Where you belong is where you are loved.'

He gazed past her into the distance, trying to avoid her eyes. Gradually he became aware that someone was waving to him. Disbelieving, he pointed at a woman in the distance. 'I know her,' he said. 'She looks a lot slimmer and younger – but it's her.'

His mother glanced round. 'Yes,' she said. 'It's Sadie. She goes climbing with me. Come and say hello.'

As Goldman approached the African woman, she ran up laughing. 'Hello, my friend,' she said. 'It's good to see you again. How was your journeying? Did you enjoy the noisy band? Those boys are good, aren't they?'

Goldman ignored the questions. 'What are you doing here? I thought you were –'

'Building my toilet?' she said with a smile. 'I'm afraid it didn't work out as I'd planned. In fact I never did get my toilet, despite your help.'

'But what went wrong?' asked Goldman uneasily.

'I'm not exactly sure. Maybe it was the boy who came to show you the way, or the man who sold me the toilet pipes, or perhaps a neighbour. But whatever it was, the news got round. It seems that someone had heard from someone else that a rich white stranger had come and given me money. A lot of money. So that I would not have to go outside to the toilet in the dark in my night clothes.'

'And what happened?' said Goldman.

'Someone came to my house. It was in the night. I heard them moving around. I got up to see who was there. I remember a movement behind me and a pain in the back of my head. And then I was on the floor. I heard the intruder searching my house. Then he ran out and it was quiet.'

'That was my fault,' said Goldman. 'If I hadn't given you the money . . .'

'No,' said Sadie firmly. 'I did not have to take the money. I was careless. I must have told someone. But, in any case, it does not matter. I thought of you as I lay there on the earth floor of my little house.'

'You must have cursed the day you met me,' said Goldman bitterly. 'I was just trying to be kind.'

She reached out and gently wiped the tears from his face. Her fingers were soft, soothing away his pain. 'No, I did not curse you,' said Sadie quietly. 'As I lay there I thought about what you had done, and how hard it must have been for you to give that money away. I thought how brave you were to do it. I can't remember clearly, but I'm sure I died smiling.'

'Smiling?' said Goldman. 'What was there to smile about? You were dying.'

'Yes,' said Sadie. 'I knew that. I was smiling at the thought that death was a small price to pay for such a loving thing to have happened to me.'

'Sadie.'

'Yes, I know. And I love you, too. But it is not something to cry about. Unless your tears are of happiness.' She looked at him kindly. 'Now go. You have important things to do.'

Goldman turned to his mother. A great weight seemed to be lifting from him. He felt taller and found he was breathing more deeply.

'Come on,' she said. 'You'll be seeing Sadie again.'

As they walked, Goldman was silent.

'Are you all right, Harry?'

'Yes. I was thinking. About Sadie. And other things.'

'Anything in particular?'

'I was thinking about when you went away,' said Goldman quietly. 'You never said goodbye.'

'My dearest, darling boy, I did say goodbye. All the way to the hospital in the ambulance and later, in the bed in the hospital ward, I never stopped saying goodbye. It's just that no one could hear me. But I loved you till the moment I died, and I've not stopped loving you since.'

Goldman hesitated. 'And then there was Dad . . . do you know about all that?'

The woman looked serious. 'Yes, I know about it,' she said gently. 'He's here, too. The last time I saw him he was in the gardens digging. He's taken to growing roses again.'

'Roses?' said Goldman, remembering the garden of his childhood.

'Yes. Never underestimate the importance of beauty, Harry.'

'I had roses back at my house, Tresco. Lots of them.'

'But did you ever take time to enjoy them?'

'No,' said Goldman, 'I suppose not.'

'Well, maybe now's the time to do that,' she said.

Mention of his father had made Goldman uneasy, as though there was a chill in the air. He changed the subject abruptly. 'So, what happens here?' he said, looking round. 'What do people do?'

His mother smiled. 'All sorts of things but, in a word, we grow.' Seeing that he was not convinced, she went on. 'OK, tell me this. What was the best part of being rich and successful? There must have been something you found attractive about it. Something that gave you a real buzz?'

'The best part was making it all happen,' said Goldman. 'Not so much the money, but building it all up from nothing. That was great.'

'Making it grow?'

'Yes.'

'Well, there you are. That's what happens here. As I said, there's always something going on. Sometimes it's like living on a construction site.'

'But so much of what I did was wrong,' said Goldman. 'I damaged people – I ruined their lives. Right up to that last morning, I was doing it. You don't know the half of what went on.'

His mother looked at him gravely. 'Yes, I do. I know exactly what happened, and I think I know why it went so wrong.'

'You do?'

She nodded. 'A lot of it was your own doing, and you've got to face up to that. In fact, you've already started facing up to it. But it wasn't all your fault. Bad things happened in the past, when you were a child. To you and to other people.'

'I was scared,' said Goldman. 'Despite all the money and power, I was still scared. I said that to Sheppard, once.'

She put a hand on his arm. 'You know what I said a few minutes ago, about rock climbing and leaving my fear back at the river? Well, that's the secret. Were you afraid when you were in the boat with Rosie and Sheppard and they tipped you into the sea?'

'I was terrified. I panicked and I started to sink.'

'And then you found out why you were sinking, and you started to float. But weren't you still afraid with half a mile of water underneath you?'

Goldman thought back to the journey in Rosie's boat and the sensation of being held up by the water. 'Yes, for a second or two, I was. But after that it felt OK. In fact it was quite exciting, although I didn't want to admit it to the others.'

His mother smiled. 'There you are. That's what it's like here. Unexpected things happen and, for an instant, you're sure you're going to be afraid. But, somehow, you're not. It's like the first time I went climbing. I lost my footing and ended up hanging in mid-air on a rope, three hundred feet up a cliff face.'

'What did you do?'

'I screamed. For an instant I thought I was afraid. But then I realized it was a good rope and I was perfectly safe.'

'You've changed,' said Goldman.

'No, I haven't. This is who I always was, underneath,' said his mother. 'I simply grew.'

'I wish I could have courage like that,' said Goldman.

'Well, now's your chance,' said his mother, as a young man walked towards them. 'Do you recognize him?'

Goldman was gripped by panic as he saw his father approaching. He remembered the dark days. A man bursting in through the door, roaring drunk. Bawling for his supper. Raging at his wife when the food didn't arrive fast enough for him. A small boy screaming in terror, shouting: 'No, Daddy, no!' And the big man taking off his belt. And the beatings that seemed to go on for ever. Then, afterwards, his mother rushed to hospital in the night and never coming back.

Even now, as the man walked towards them across the grass, Goldman wanted to run away and hide, but his mother was gripping his arm firmly.

'Face it, Harry,' she said quietly.

'What shall I do?'

'Grow,' she said.

He was not sure what happened next.

As the man approached, Goldman felt like a small child again. He braced himself for the blows he knew would come. Instead, the man took his hand. 'I'm sorry,' said his father. 'I'm so sorry.'

Years of anger and bitterness seemed to evaporate. Goldman thought back to the fields of death and the cries of recognition and greeting that carried faintly across the frozen earth. It was as though his own grave was being opened. A nightmare was ending.

'I'm sorry,' said his father again. 'I messed things up. Badly. Things happened at the pit. Men were laid off. Lives wasted – destroyed, some of them. We were so angry. I took it out on you.'

He paused. 'I've no right to ask this, but can you forgive me?'

Goldman was about to say, 'It doesn't matter,' but then realized with a sense of shock that it did matter. It mattered hugely. The pain and the suffering were real and would remain real. He took a deep breath. 'I do forgive you.'

He was surprised that the words didn't sound ridiculous. They were simply a statement of fact, although at that moment 'forgiveness' didn't seem quite the right word. All he knew was that he loved his dad.

He was conscious that something was happening. As though a key was turning silently in a lock. A door was opening. He felt lightheaded. If he could forgive his father, then . . .

Goldman realized that his mother was watching intently.

'Was that OK?' he asked, embarrassed.

'You did very well,' she said. 'You were very brave. I'm proud of you both.'

'What are you smiling about?' said Goldman.

'You boys,' she said. 'And how much I love you. And about something else.'

'What else is there?'

'That when you open your heart to forgive, you open your heart to be forgiven.'

* * *

'This is all taking a bit of getting used to,' said Goldman later.

'There's no hurry,' said his mother. 'Just enjoy being here. Then, when the time is right, you need to think what you would most like to do.'

'I can tell you that now,' said Goldman. 'I want to build a boat. A little boat, like Rosie's. Build it with my own hands and sail it on my own, like she does. And swimming. I want to learn to swim.'

The song of your soul

As they walked, Goldman noticed a stillness in the air. People paused in their conversations expectantly. Nothing was quite normal.

Then Goldman realized that the ground beneath his feet was trembling. There was a low rumbling that grew louder. The sound was now a pounding roar in his head. The ground was shaking, as if they were caught in an earthquake. He looked round in alarm, remembering the flood that had destroyed the squatter camp. Across the open landscape, he could make out a low cloud of dust that spanned the horizon. It looked like a vast tidal wave rushing towards him. Even at that distance the sight was frightening.

Out of the dust storm, he could make out a thundering mass of horses and riders. And in the centre, a point of brilliant light. The sound was deafening. Overwhelming. Goldman covered his face with his hands. His whole body was shaking like the ground beneath his feet as the horses raced towards him. He realized that nothing could stop them.

He was filled with a deep foreboding as he waited for the impact. The tearing of flesh as he was trampled to death. Crushed beneath the hooves like a fly on a window. But, strangely, now that it had come to the ending of it all, he felt released.

I shall not return again, he thought. I shall not return. What the words meant he did not know, but they did not make him unhappy.

He was glad that he had seen his mother and made things right with his father. Glad that he had received Sadie's forgiveness, and that he had seen the boy with the scrap of blue cloth grow to glorious manhood.

But what of beloved Sheppard? He regretted that there had been no time for a proper farewell; a chance to thank him for being such a good companion on their long, long journey. To thank him for being such a true friend.

As he waited for those last moments to pass, he was grateful that there would not be any ice. 'There was no ice,' the man in the crowd had said. He was not sure what was happening but, hopefully, there would be no eternal punishment in the freezing depths of hell.

He tried to cry out with thanks, but found that he was spinning, turning . . . floating. Until there was utter silence.

Nothing moved. It was as though he had fallen into a deep slumber.

Slowly, he opened his eyes. Above him, terrifyingly close, stood a magnificent horse. Its chestnut-brown coat glistened in the sun and he could feel its warm breath on his face. Sitting astride the beautiful creature was Rosie.

'You made it!' she said, leaping down. She flung her arms round him and he felt the strength of her embrace. For a moment he thought he could hear singing. Her skin was warm like the sun and her hair soft against his face.

'What is that?' he whispered. 'I can hear music.'

'The song of your soul, dear friend,' she murmured. 'The song of your soul.'

Now others were crowding round in a chatter of excitement.

Rosie stepped back, her hands on his shoulders. Holding him at arm's length, she looked searchingly into his eyes. 'It's good to have you here,' she said.

He opened his mouth to speak, but Rosie put her fingers against his lips. 'Say nothing. Just know that you are welcome. All is well. Trust me – all is well.'

'But the things I did,' said Goldman. 'All that crap. What about all that . . . ?'

'Is that all you were?' said Rosie, a hard edge in her voice. 'A list of things you did? Was there nothing more? Or were you also loved? By your mother and your sister, and even by your father? By a tramp at your gate? And by people in another place? You were always a loved person – and that is what you are.' She paused, then added thoughtfully, 'And I have something for you.'

She held out her hand and Goldman saw that it was an old photograph. A picture of a child in a cot, covered with a small blue blanket. The photograph had been torn in pieces, but someone had carefully stuck it together again with adhesive tape.

'Where did you get that?' he said. The words seemed to echo in his head.

'From a friend. Someone who used to clean the house for you back at Tresco. The woman who befriended Trudi. She found it one day in the wastepaper basket in your office. She wanted you to have it.'

'But why?' said Goldman.

'Because it's important,' said Rosie. 'It's a part of who you are. It's a reminder that even when you throw things away, nothing is ever lost. Neither the image of your child, nor you yourself, Harry.'

'But he was lost,' said Goldman. 'I lost him.'

'And then he found you. But you didn't recognize him.'

He looked into her eyes. There was a depth of wisdom in them that made him almost afraid.

Rosie kissed him lightly on both cheeks. 'Nothing is ever lost,' she whispered. 'Remember that.'

Then she leapt back on to the horse. She looked across the river to where Sheppard stood talking to Raffa. Putting her fingers to her lips, she gave a piercing whistle. The sound echoed powerfully across the water.

Goldman wished that he had learned to whistle like that. It would have been so good in the playground at school. He had been small and plump and bullied. Yes, to have been able to whistle like that would have been good. Perhaps things might have turned out differently.

On the other side of the river, Sheppard turned and looked back at Rosie. He raised his arm in salutation.

'I gave you the frog,' she called out. 'You gave me back the prince.'

There was a roar of laughter from the crowd.

Rosie turned back to Goldman, looking intently down into his eyes. 'Remember,' she said gravely. 'You are yourself. You are much loved, and you are welcome here.' She grinned. 'And one day I will teach you how to whistle like that.'

She kicked her bare feet against the flanks of the horse, and they were gone.

Goldman looked round at the others, wiping the wetness from his face with the back of his hand. In the grass were the marks the horse's hooves had cut into the turf. Her laughter seemed to hang in the still air.

He shaded his eyes to see where the horse and rider were, but they had already disappeared into the glare of the sun. He touched his face where Rosie had kissed him; then caught his mother's eye. She smiled. 'It's all right. You're safe. You're home now.'

'And what about Rosie?'

His mother frowned for a moment. 'That young woman just never stops working,' she said. 'Always on the go.'

With his arms around his father and mother he felt completely, gloriously alive. He wanted to tell Sheppard how he felt. And something else. Goldman looked across the river, and saw him deep in conversation with Raffa. Somewhere in the far distance, or perhaps in the back of his mind, Goldman thought he heard the merest hint of a song. 'There's something I need to do,' he said abruptly.

'There's nothing you need to do, Harry,' said his mother.

He thought for a moment. 'You're right. I don't need to do it. But I want to do it, more than anything else. I want to go and ask Sheppard something. Don't worry – I'll be back.'

'What's happening, Harry?'

'I don't quite know, but it feels good. Better than I ever felt before.'

He kissed his parents and ran back down the sloping grass towards the river.

'Harry!' called his mother. 'Why are you running? You've never run anywhere in your life.'

Goldman skidded to a halt and turned. 'I don't know why,' he shouted, throwing his arms wide. 'Maybe it's because I'm happy.'

Sheppard and Raphael looked up at Goldman's noisy approach. Instead of walking on the stepping stones, he had plunged into the water and was wading across, kicking up great showers of spray like a child playing in the sea. 'I'm back,' he announced, as he emerged dripping from the river.

'We can see that,' said Sheppard cautiously. 'But why are you back? What's wrong?'

'Nothing's wrong. I just wanted to know what you were up to.'

Sheppard and Raphael looked at each other.

'I have a few things to do,' said Sheppard evasively.

'That's what I figured,' said Goldman. 'And I'm coming with you.'

'I'm not sure that's a good idea.'

'It's a great idea,' said Goldman, grinning. 'You might need me.'

'Need you?'

'Well, maybe.' Goldman paused. 'I could help. Honestly, I could . . . Please?'

'Why do you want to help?'

'I'm not sure. I just do.'

'You're all wet,' said Sheppard.

'I don't care. Wet is good,' said Goldman, grinning.

Sheppard looked across at Raffa and sighed. 'This is the man who hates water.'

'Not any more,' said Raffa.

'What am I going to do with him?'

'Don't ask me,' said Raffa. 'You're the boss.'

* * *

The two of them walked in silence for a long time.

'Wishing you hadn't come?' said Sheppard, eventually.

'Not at all,' said Goldman. 'It feels good. Like I'm really alive.'

'Well, something's going on in that head of yours. What is it?'

'I was thinking that you've got a lot of explaining to do.'

'About what?'

'About all this.'

'Oh, we can talk about that later,' said Sheppard with a grin. 'Anyway, that's not what's bugging you. What's really on your mind?'

'It's nothing,' said Goldman, after a moment's pause.

'Are you sure?'

'Well . . . It's just that, back there, I thought –'

'You thought what?' said Sheppard, stopping and turning to face his friend.

'Back there, across the river, at the end of it all, I wondered whether there might have been . . . you know. It's what we were taught when we were kids.'

'And was what happened less than that?'

'Listen,' said Goldman grasping Sheppard's arm. 'I'm not complaining – you've got to believe that. All I'm saying is that I somehow thought there might have been – at the end of it all. Meeting your maker . . . that sort of thing.'

Sheppard grinned. 'And instead of that there was only the celestial Rosie?'

He turned and carried on walking.

Goldman stood in confusion. 'Rosie?'

Sheppard continued walking.

A thought began to dawn on Goldman. 'Sheppard,' he yelled at his friend's retreating back. 'Sheppard. You're not . . . Are you saying that Rosie was . . . ?'

Sheppard raised a hand but did not turn round.

Goldman's legs felt weak. He remembered Rosie's strong arms around him, her eyes deep with wisdom and authority. And something else. Powerful, uncompromising love. A love bursting with energy and ringing with laughter: the love that summons up the wind and hurls a small boat across the waves in a shower of sunlit spray. A love that holds the stars in timeless, silent motion. A love that is nothing less than life itself.

Ahead, down the path, Sheppard smiled to himself as he heard Goldman's great shout of laughter.

'Feeling good?' he asked when Goldman caught up with him.

'Great. Never felt better,' said Goldman, panting like a large dog.

'Well, make the most of it,' said Sheppard.

'Why? What's happening?'

'Didn't you read the small print?'

'What small print?' said Goldman.

'The bit about love.'

'And?'

'There being no love without justice.'

'I'd managed to figure that out,' said Goldman.

'And there's no justice without a struggle.'

'And?'

'That means trouble.'

'Trouble who for?' asked Goldman.

'For whom.'

'OK. For whom?'

'Don't ask. Just keep walking.'